A THIEF IN THE NIGHT

Alec and Veronica Guest are a happily married couple, living in the quiet and picturesque village of Maddingleigh. Hitherto their existence has been a peaceful one, with little to disturb the daily routine of Alec commuting each day to his solicitors' practice in the nearby town of Gaysbrook, and Veronica tending to house and garden.

Then one of their friends, Vic Ordway, a local antique dealer, has a valuable old clock stolen. Not that serious an incident, the Guests believe, but it turns out to be only the prelude to an increasingly sinister series of events which are to culminate in murder. Is the death connected to the stolen clock, or does it have more to do with the arrival of the Guests' new neighbour, the beautiful, enigmatic Nina Elvin?

With the rural tranquillity of Maddingleigh rudely shattered and the community living in suspicion and fear, will the killer in their midst be discovered before a second murder is committed?

A THIEF IN
THE NIGHT

Elizabeth Ferrars

HarperCollins*Publishers*

Collins Crime
An imprint of HarperCollins*Publishers*
77−85 Fulham Palace Road, London W6 8JB

First published in Great Britain
in 1995 by Collins Crime

1 3 5 7 9 10 8 6 4 2

© M.D. Brown 1995

The Author asserts the moral right to be
identified as the author of this work

A catalogue record for this book is
available from the British Library
ISBN 0 00 232529 2

Set in Meridien and Bodoni

Photoset by Rowland Phototypesetting Ltd
Bury St Edmunds, Suffolk
Printed and bound in Great Britain by
HarperCollinsManufacturing Glasgow

A THIEF
IN THE NIGHT

CHAPTER 1

When the scream of the police siren went past our house the time was about a quarter past eleven. I was in the kitchen, peeling potatoes. I was going to make a goulash for dinner in the evening and was doing some preparing in advance. As far as I thought of the siren at all, I thought that it was probably on an ambulance, wondered for a moment who up the road had become suddenly so ill as to need one so urgently, then put the potatoes in a saucepan, filled it with water and put it on one side of the stove. Then I got to work on peeling some onions.

It was about half an hour later that I went into the sitting-room. Alec, my husband, was there, lying on a sofa with his feet up, reading *The Times*. He does not go to his office on a Saturday. He is a solicitor and is a partner in the firm of Hollybrook, Darby, Guest, whose offices are in the town of Gaysbrook, about ten miles from the village of Maddingleigh, where we had lived for the last fifteen years. Perhaps I should say that he is the Guest in the firm, and that both he and I are fifty-one, and that we got married when we were twenty-three and he had just been taken on as a very junior clerk in the firm.

We lived in Gaysbrook in those days. My job as a librarian helped out, and we had a very pleasant flat, but when a number of years later he became a partner in the firm we bought the house in Maddingleigh on which we had had an eye for some time. It had just come on the market and as soon as we discovered this, we made an offer for it, bought it and moved in and had never regretted it.

I had given up my job some time before and living in the country found that gardening more than filled my time. The house was of grey Cotswold stone, with a roof of old red tiles, and dated from the seventeenth century. But other owners before us had done what they could to increase its comfort. It had central heating, a modern kitchen with fridge and freezer, and two quite elegant bathrooms. Except for a certain amount of redecorating we had done very little to it ourselves and by degrees had acquired furniture that it seemed to us belonged there. We had bought a good deal of this from an antique dealer whose shop was in Gaysbrook, but who, like us, had a house in Maddingleigh. He was a near neighbour of ours, and we were engaged to visit him that morning for drinks at twelve o'clock. He was a very sociable man and I believe knew everybody in the village.

As I came into the sitting-room another siren started screaming in the lane that went past our house. I went to the window and saw a white and blue car shoot past our gate.

'Police,' I said.

Alec grunted.

'What can have happened?' I asked.

'A murder, probably,' came from behind *The Times*.

'No, but really . . . ?'

The point was that our lane has very few houses along it. It winds through farmlands and orchards till it joins one of the main roads into Gaysbrook. There is a pub at the corner where it does this called the Green Man, a sophisticated place where you could have very good lunches and dinners and buy excellent takeaway meals, but there were not many places to which it seemed probable the police could be called so urgently.

'Accident in the main road, I should say,' Alec said.

I agreed that that was likely, but I went on standing at the window, which was small, set deep in thick walls, half expecting to see a third police car, or perhaps an ambulance, go careering past. I was wondering where the cars had come from. We have a constable in Maddingleigh who has a car, but I found it hard to imagine him involved in such a chase. That was foolish of me. When duty called, he could no doubt drive with the best of them. It was just that I had never seen his car out on the road. It seemed always to be placidly parked in front of the cottage where he lived in the village.

But though there were no more police cars or sirens just then there was something else that held my attention as I looked out of the window. A removal van was standing in front of the house opposite ours and two or three men were lounging near it, as if waiting to be told what to do. The house had been empty for some months, but, as I knew, had recently been sold. It was a bungalow and was the only modern building along the lane. At the time when it had been built, about five years ago, there had been protests by local people at such a thing being allowed, but an appeal by the ones who had bought the land on which it stood had been successful and the building had gone ahead.

It was L-shaped, with a carport with room for two cars and was really not unattractive. It was white, with big windows, a roof of grey pantiles and a green front door. But the people who had built it had never really settled in there and about a year ago had put it on the market. The boom in house property was over and it had taken some time to sell, but as soon as this had been achieved they had departed for New Zealand. Seeing the van, I assumed our new neighbour would shortly be appearing, and lingered at the window for a few minutes to see, but nothing happened.

It struck me as I stood there that it was time I put some

weedkiller on the gravel in front of the house. It is a fair-sized expanse, with an oval rose-bed in the middle of it, and a low stone wall with a wide gate in it bordering the lane. I must buy the weedkiller, I thought, the next time I went into Gaysbrook. It was unlikely that the one store in the village would stock it, though it supplied almost everything that an ordinary household needed. Meanwhile, I thought, I might as well be getting on with preparing the bread and butter pudding that I intended for our evening meal, and I was turning away to go to the kitchen when a car, which I later discovered was a Mercedes, drew up behind the removal van.

My curiosity aroused, I lingered at the window, and saw a woman get out of the car. I knew it would be a woman, because I had been told by her brother, Raymond Markham, who had lived in the village for some years, that his sister had bought the house, her divorce having at last been made absolute. It had been a divorce that had not been one of the amiable, good-mannered sort, in which both parties are relieved to be free and think kindly of one another, but bitter and destructive. I had been told a good deal about her by Raymond and his wife Marianne, but although she had occasionally visited them, I had never met her.

'There's our new neighbour arriving,' I said. 'If we weren't going out ourselves, I'd ask her in for a drink.'

'Hell!' Alec exclaimed. 'I'd forgotten we were going out.'

'Well, you'd better wake up, because we'll have to be setting off fairly soon,' I said.

'Have we really got to go?' he asked. 'Why can't people leave us in peace?'

'You know you want to go, so don't be silly. Come and look at our neighbour.'

He got up, but folded the newspaper carefully before he joined me, so carefully, indeed, as he always did when

he had been reading it, that our neighbour had disappeared into her house before he joined me. But he had
not missed much. All that I had seen of her as she went
to her door was that she was tall and slim, with blonde
hair to her shoulders, and was wearing slacks and a
sweater and carrying a shoulder-bag. I had had hardly a
glimpse of her face. Anyway, at that distance, even if she
had looked towards me, I should not have been able to
distinguish much. I knew from her brother Raymond that
she was twenty-nine and had a child, a girl, I believed.

She was not to be seen when presently Alec and I set
out for our friend's house. The men whom I had seen
waiting for her by the van were handling into the house
a piece of furniture which I thought was part of a tallboy.
It took us about ten minutes to reach our destination. Alec
insisted on strolling very slowly, otherwise we could have
reached it in half the time. He was in one of his anti-social
moods, and his face, which is really very good-looking,
had an absent, brooding expression. He is tall, wide-
shouldered but bony, slightly stooping and with a casual,
loose-limbed way of walking. What hair he has left is dark,
but it has receded a long way from his forehead, which
as a result looks very high and rather distinguished. He
has arched dark eyebrows and dark eyes which, when he
allows it, can be very expressive. His nose is long and thin
and his cheeks hollow. He can look very severe, or almost
boyishly cheerful and friendly.

'I suppose you'll be asking her in before long,' he said
as we passed the bungalow. 'Why couldn't the place just
stay empty? It was very peaceful.'

'You don't think she's actually going to wreck your
peace, do you?' I answered. 'What are you afraid of?
Rowdy parties? Unwelcome intrusion? If she turns on the
radio too loud, we're hardly likely to hear it at that distance, even if she leaves all her windows open. Anyway,

you may find you like her very much when you get to know her.'

'I'm afraid you'll be asking her in at all hours, and I'll have to stay up in the bedroom if I just want a little quiet.'

'You really like quiet much less than I do. But actually I was thinking of asking her in for a cup of tea this afternoon. Moving into a new house is a messy and exhausting business. A cup of tea could be welcome.'

'What do you actually know about her?' he asked.

'Only what Raymond and Marianne have told me. That her name's Nina Elvin, but that she's thinking of going back to her own name, which of course is Markham, that the husband she's divorced is a journalist and was unfaithful and cruel, but that she's got money of her own from a first marriage and is really very well-off and that she's got one child. Is that enough to be going on with?'

'What happened to the first husband?'

'I'm not sure, but I think he died.'

'She isn't very likely to pick up a third in Maddingleigh. Very few people here are under sixty.'

'There's ourselves,' I said. 'We're only fifty-one. And the Markhams are in their thirties.'

'We're the exceptions.'

'Actually, there are probably plenty of young people here, only we just don't mix with them. But it may really explain why she's come here. She may have had enough of marriage.'

Alec gave a sudden laugh and put an arm round my shoulders.

'I'm sorry. I don't know what's got into me. Let's ask her in for tea.'

We walked a little faster after that.

The friend whom we were going to visit, Victor Ordway, lived about halfway between our house and the Green Man, in a house that was even older than ours. It was thatched, with plenty of dark beams showing in its white walls and small, square windows with diamond panes. It had once been a farmhouse and had several old barns alongside it which had been turned into garages and workshops, where Vic, as we called him, did a good deal of the repair work on things that later appeared in his shop in Gaysbrook. The house had no front garden but a door that opened straight on to the road. It stood open at the moment, for Vic had visitors. Two police cars stood nose to tail in front of the house.

It made us hesitate. If Vic was having trouble with the police our visit might be a nuisance. On the other hand, it might be helpful.

'Come on,' Alec said. 'He could have phoned us if he didn't want us to come.'

We skirted the cars, reached the open door and Alec gave it a resounding knock with the old black knocker.

It was answered at once by Tom Forster, the constable who lived in the village. He was a big, burly man with a large round face and bristling yellow hair. It looked as if he was quite glad to see us. He said good morning, then added, 'A bad business this.'

'What's happened?' Alec asked.

'Burglary,' Tom Forster answered. 'Valuable clock's been stolen.'

'A valuable clock!' I exclaimed. 'Not the Tompion!'

'Yes, the Tompion!' Vic cried out, emerging from behind Tom. 'Gone! Clean gone!'

He was a small man of about fifty-five, very lightly built, with wide shoulders and long arms which gave him a little the look of an oversized monkey. There was a touch of the monkey too about his face, with its flat nose, wide mouth and wide grey-green eyes. His hair was light brown and stood straight up from his low forehead and generally had the look of needing cutting, not because he intended to wear it long as was fashionable, but simply because he could not be bothered to go to the barber. He was wearing

13

brown corduroy trousers, an orange pullover, brightly patterned socks and sandals. He looked excited and distraught
and eager to pour his heart out.

'Come in! Come in!' he cried. 'I'm glad you came. When
I telephoned – but I didn't, did I? – I was going to tele-
phone you to put you off, but I forgot, and now I'm glad
I did. It's good to see you. Yes, the Tompion's gone.'

Tom Forster had moved away from the doorway and
we had stepped into the passage that ran from the front
to the back of the house and the first thing that struck me
as we did so was the empty space facing us where the
valuable old clock had stood. I knew nothing about clocks,
but Vic had always been ready to talk about it, so I knew
that it had been made in the seventeenth century and that
it was a mistake to call it a grandfather clock. It was a
longcase clock. I believed that Vic had inherited it from
his father, who had been a collector of clocks and from
whom Vic presumably had also inherited his passion for
antiques. Most of his collection had vanished bit by bit in
the shop in Gaysbrook, but he had always treasured the
Tompion and kept it in his home.

'Come in and meet Inspector Frayne,' he said, shepherd-
ing us into his sitting-room, where we found a man sitting
at a table with one hand just reaching out for the telephone. There was another man in the room, standing by
the window. Both were in uniform. The inspector abandoned the telephone as we came into the room and stood
up and Vic introduced us.

'My friends, Mr and Mrs Guest – Inspector Frayne from
Gaysbrook. Perhaps I should have told you I was expecting
them for drinks, Inspector, but I clean forgot they were
coming.'

As Alec had forgotten that we were supposed to come,
it looked as if it had been very much a matter of chance
that we had actually met that morning.

14

The inspector said, 'Good morning. I wonder if it's just possible you can help me.'

He was a tall, well-made man of about forty, with a long face with strong, rather heavy features and very bright blue eyes. The other man in the room was much younger, probably not more than thirty, and I thought he was a sergeant.

'I'd be glad to help,' Alec said, 'but I don't even know what's happened, except that I gather the Tompion's been stolen. I'm sorry, Vic. I know how you treasured it.'

'It's abominable!' Vic exclaimed. 'Atrocious! And d'you realize that whoever took it must be someone who's come into the house as a friend, because it isn't every Tom, Dick and Harry, I mean the plumber, or the decorator or the window-cleaner, who'd know the value of the thing. And it's someone who knew I was going to be in London for the last couple of days.'

'That's going a bit fast, Mr Ordway,' the inspector said. 'Your Tom, Dick or Harry may not have known much about clocks himself, but he may have talked casually to someone who did, who managed to deduce what you'd got here, and perhaps even came and took a look at it when you were out. On the other hand, of course, you may be right and we'll be looking into that very carefully. And we'll look into this question of who knew you were going to London, but I'm afraid more people than you'd think of may have done so. Anyone going into your shop, for instance, and happening to ask your assistant where you were.'

'Now don't get suspicious of Giles!' Vic said fiercely. 'He's worked for me for four years and he's as honest as the day.'

'No doubt, no doubt,' the inspector said, 'but he could have given the information quite innocently.'

'Only to someone who knew me. He wouldn't have given the information to all and sundry.'

15

'When did this thing happen?' Alec asked. 'Last night, was it?'

'Ah, I was just going to ask you if you could tell us anything about that,' the inspector said. 'Did you happen to notice anything unusual – any stranger, perhaps, or a van that didn't seem to you to belong here – at any time last night?'

Alec shook his head.

Inspector Frayne turned to me. 'Mrs Guest?'

'The only thing that's struck me as strange since yesterday,' I said, 'were the sirens of your cars. This isn't a busy road. It isn't full of traffic that might hold you up.'

'True,' he said, 'but there was a big removal van a little way down it, half blocking it, with several men standing around, and it was simply a warning to them that made us use the sirens.'

'A removal van,' Vic said with interest. 'Then Mrs Elvin's moving in?'

'It looks like it,' I said.

'Have you met her?'

But the inspector seemed to feel that this was straying off the important matter under discussion.

'We'll be looking for fingerprints, of course,' he said, 'but I don't expect we'll find anything. This has the look of a professional job. They won't have been careless.'

'Oh, it was professional all right,' Vic agreed. 'When you're moving a Tompion you don't just pick it up and carry it along. It has to be taken to some extent to pieces. Whoever masterminded this affair last night, there was someone there who knew plenty about clocks.'

'But you've no suspicion who that might have been?'

'None at all.'

'You're sure it happened last night, are you?' Alec said.

'Well, according to Mr Ordway, he was away for two nights,' the inspector said, 'so the house was empty since Thursday, but there's one piece of evidence that suggests

16

the theft happened last night. It rained in the night for the first time since last weekend and there are muddy tyre-marks in one of the garages, the sort of tyre-marks that a van would make. By itself that may not mean much, but it's suggestive.'

'I think it's more than suggestive, it's conclusive,' Vic said. 'Now, if your fingerprint gang are going to be arriving soon, d'you want us around? I was thinking that if you didn't actually need us, we might go up to the Green Man for the drinks for which I invited my friends. It seems to me we'll only be in your way if we stay here and you'll know where to find us if you need us.'

The inspector seemed to think it would be quite a good thing if we were not under his feet when the fingerprint people arrived. The house was a small one and it would be very difficult for us to keep out of their way. So he indicated that we were welcome to go to the Green Man and we stepped out into the road and set off towards it.

The Green Man is a square, redbrick Victorian building which stands at the corner where our lane joins the main road to Gaysbrook. It was only a few minutes from Vic's house. I should perhaps have mentioned that Vic was unmarried and lived alone. One of the village women came in twice a week to clean the house, but he cooked for himself when he did not eat in Gaysbrook, coped with his dishwasher and did his own shopping. I had heard that he had been married for a time when he was young, but he never talked about it. Whether divorce or death had put an end to it I did not know, or indeed for certain whether or not it had ever really happened. He was the kind of man who it seems only natural should live alone, not in the least because he was an isolated sort of person but rather the reverse, too involved with too many people to be able to make a choice, or to give his heart to any single person.

We did not talk much as we walked towards the Green Man, except that he told us that he had gone to London to attend a sale at which he had been fortunate enough to buy some Georgian silver.

'They sent me a catalogue and there was something that I especially wanted,' he said. 'A George I lemon-strainer, a lovely thing. But I didn't get it. The price went too high for me. But I got a George III swing-basket, silver, you know, with open-work sides and a blue glass lining. I thought I was really in luck, getting it, but now it simply doesn't seem to matter. I grew up with that old Tompion. Next to certain human beings there's nothing I've ever cared for so much.'

'It was insured, I assume,' Alec said as we pushed open the door of the lounge bar of the Green Man and went up to the bar to order our drinks.

'Thank the Lord, yes!' Vic said. 'I've told myself over and over again that I couldn't afford the premiums, but I always kept them going. I don't insure the stuff in the shop. I couldn't afford it and I don't think there's too much risk. But we're pretty isolated out here and as we've just found out, thefts are only too easy. But I meant what I said to that policeman, you know, whoever took that clock knew all about it and a good deal about me.'

He bought a sherry for me, a whisky and water for Alec and beer for himself. Then he suggested that we might have sandwiches, as for him at least lunch at home, if not quite impossible to prepare in the midst of all the policemen, was not an attractive prospect.

'But I suppose I'd better not be away too long,' he said as we went towards a table in a bay window with our drinks and sandwiches. 'I'd like to keep away for the rest of the day, but it wouldn't be judicious.'

The bar was long and narrow, with panelled walls and chequered linoleum on the floor. There were not many people there, but one of them, an electrician who on several occasions had done work for us, knew Vic and accosted him.

'You in any trouble, Mr Ordway?' he said as we were passing the table where he sat with his wife. 'I see you got the police in.'

'Only a burglary,' Vic answered. 'No dead bodies around.'

'That's something,' the man said. 'But did they get away with anything valuable?'

'Just a clock,' Vic said. 'A rather rare old clock.'

'Rare, was it? That's bad. I'm sorry. But it could have been worse, couldn't it? But I'm really sorry, Mr Ordway.'

'Thanks, Ben,' Vic said. 'But there's always a chance we'll get it back.'

'That's right. That's the way to think of it. Remember how Pat Channing got his car stolen and got it back in a couple of days.'

Pat Channing was the owner of the village store.

As we sat down at our table Alec said, 'Is there a chance you might get it back, Vic?'

'Not a hope in hell, I should say,' Vic answered. 'It isn't as if it'll ever appear on the open market. It was stolen by someone who wanted just that particular clock and has a home waiting for it, or if he didn't do the job himself, then by someone who knew he had a customer ready to buy it.'

'What's its value, approximately?' Alec asked.

'About eighty thousand, I should say.'

Alec gave a little whistle.

Vic added, 'It's really something very special, you know, even among Tompions.'

'Then it's lucky you kept up with the premiums.'

'Oh yes, and I may even be glad of it all in the end. Things haven't been going too well with me recently. I've occasionally even thought of selling the clock, but I couldn't bring myself to think about it seriously.'

For all the time that we had known Vic, which was for a number of years, things, according to him, had not been going well for him. Yet the shop in Gaysbrook always had an opulent air and allowing for the fact that he looked after it himself, except for the help of his friend Giles, he seemed in a quiet way to live luxuriously, so we had never taken him seriously.

He struck the table now with a clenched fist. 'The fact is, I'm so angry, I can hardly talk about it! If I ever find out who did it –' He broke off with a startled look on his face.

A young man had just come into the bar and was buying a whisky for himself. He looked about thirty, and was tall and very thin, with narrow shoulders and narrow hips so that he made me think absurdly for a moment of an exclamation mark. His head was small, on a long neck, with plentiful dark brown hair which he wore rather long, not out of casualness as Vic wore his, but because that was how he liked it. His face was long and narrow with a sharply pointed nose and close-set brown eyes. He was wearing jeans and a loose black and white sweater.

Seeing Vic, he made a little gesture of greeting to him with one hand, then went and sat down by himself on a bench in a corner of the bar.

Vic called out to him, 'Come on, you may as well join us.' It did not sound very inviting and Vic's forehead had creased into an unfriendly frown. As the young man got up from his bench and came towards us, he added, 'What are *you* doing here? I shouldn't have thought this was the place for you.'

'There are still a few things to settle,' the stranger said. 'Easiest to do on the spot.'

Vic turned to Alec and me.

'Let me introduce Nigel Elvin, ex-husband of your new neighbour. Nigel, these are my friends Veronica and Alec Guest. They occupy the house just opposite the bungalow that your wife has bought. I've been told she's moving in today. Have you and she decided to do things in a friendly way after all?'

Nigel Elvin sat down at our table.

'She's got some things of mine,' he said. 'They've been in store ever since we gave up our flat. Books, mainly. She could have sent them to me, but she doesn't answer my letters when I write to her. So the easiest thing seemed to be to come and get them. I heard from Raymond that she was moving into her new place today. Raymond's been useful. We never liked each other much, but he's got sense enough to want to tidy things up decently.'

It surprised me that this long, thin man with his long, thin face and sharply pointed features was curiously good-looking. At least he was distinctive. But he was looking at Vic with a strange watchfulness, as if he was wondering what Vic was likely to do next, which was puzzling. He took no notice at all of Alec or me.

He went on inevitably, 'The police seem interested in a house down the road. D'you know anything about it?'

'As it's my house, I do,' Vic said, and went on to tell Nigel Elvin of the theft of the Tompion.

'Bad show,' he said, still with his intent gaze on Vic's face. 'You were away in London, you say?'

'Yes, I went up for a couple of nights,' Vic answered. 'I went to a couple of sales, had dinner last night with some friends, then came down here this morning. I arrived about half past ten. First thing I saw on getting in, naturally, was that the Tompion was missing. I phoned the police and they came fairly quickly. But I'm only just beginning to get used to the fact that the old thing's gone. I loved that clock. It meant more to me than all my other possessions put together.'

'Where d'you stay when you go up to London like that?' Nigel Elvin asked. 'Is there any special place you go to?'

It seemed to me a remarkably irrelevant question, but

Elvin went on, 'I'm still looking for somewhere to stay. Since I left the flat I've moved about a dozen times. I'm in Highgate at the moment. Not that I suppose you can tell me anything useful.'

'Why don't you get yourself another flat?' Vic answered. 'It's what you'll have to do in the end.'

'I've got a flat,' Elvin said, 'only no furniture except what I've borrowed. And I've not all that much money. But where did you stay?'

The question seemed to irritate Vic. The deep lines reappeared across his forehead.

'Some place in Bloomsbury,' he said. 'I forget the name of it. Not too bad and reasonably inexpensive.'

'D'you go up by car or train?' Elvin asked.

Again, it seemed to me a rather strange question to ask.

'By car,' Vic said, looking as if he regretted having invited the young man to join us. 'You came by car yourself, I suppose.'

'Since I'm hoping to collect some of my property and take it away with me, yes, naturally.'

'And are you staying here, or going back to London today?'

'I expect I'm staying. I've booked a room here in this pub. Nina won't part with even a number of books she doesn't want without a fair amount of argument. That place where you stayed in Bloomsbury, is it Garnish's Hotel, in Bolt Street?'

'I believe so, yes. Yes, that's it.'

It seemed to cost Vic an effort to admit it, as if perhaps the hotel were a more squalid sort of place than he wanted Alec and me to know he frequented. It seemed stupid, but there was altogether something a bit strange about the whole conversation between him and Elvin. It could hardly matter to Elvin where Vic had spent his two nights in London. Yet Vic looked as if it did matter.

I began to wonder how Vic and Elvin had got to know

22

one another. I supposed it was through the Markhams, in the days when he and his wife had been at least fairly peaceably married, but we ourselves had never met him at the Markhams' house. Yet he and Vic seemed to know each other moderately well. In their conversation, which struck me as far from friendly, there was a sound of intimacy which even if it did not go very deep, was at least close enough for them to probe into matters that really concerned neither of them, but that irritated them both. I was thankful that Elvin drank his whisky quickly and did not linger. But when he had left us Vic fell silent, staring straight before him with a worried look on his face.

'Sorry about that,' he said after a moment. 'I shouldn't have asked him over.'

'He's a journalist, isn't he?' Alec said. 'Someone told me that.'

'Freelance. Mostly travel stuff. Queer sort of bloke. Never could stay in any settled job. I think that was one of the things Nina couldn't stand about him. She wanted stability. And then the other woman turned up – more than one other woman, to go by what I've heard. Anyway, I'm sure she's well out of things.'

'She divorced him, didn't she, not the other way round?'

'Oh yes, and she'd no need to worry about the financial side of things. Her first husband left her quite a wealthy woman. Raymond's told me all about it. Now, I'm sorry to hurry you, but I think I ought to get back as soon as I can. But actually there's no need for you to leave. Let me get you another drink before I go.'

We decided, however, to leave when he did, and after a short time the three of us set off down the road towards our two houses. The police cars were still outside Vic's when we reached it and parted with him.

As we walked on, Alec observed, 'That young man wasn't Vic's favourite person, was he? I wonder why. Not that I took to him very warmly myself. But what did you make of him?'

'Well, for some reason I can't help thinking of something absurdly irrelevant,' I said. 'And it's nothing to do with the young man. It's the question of why Vic needed two days in London to go to his sale. He told us what he was doing there yesterday, but nothing about the day before. He did say he spent two days in London, didn't he?'

'Yes, but I don't see why he should have told us about what he was doing. He may have been visiting friends or relations, or going to the theatre or a concert, or anything. There may even be a woman there.'

'Yes, I know. I know it's nothing to do with us.'

'It's sad about the clock though, isn't it? He really cared for it.'

'Do you think he's right that it must have been taken by someone he knew quite well?'

'It's possible.'

'But not awfully probable?'

'I don't know about that. There are probably lots of people in his own line who knew that he had the thing. He's a hospitable character. He's probably asked any number of them home at different times when they'll have seen it.'

'And one of them knew that he'd be away from home last night?'

'That's more of a puzzle.'

We had reached our gate. The removal van was still outside the bungalow opposite and so was the tall, slim woman of whom I had had a glimpse earlier. She was talking to one of the removal men, signing something for which he seemed to be waiting, and it seemed only right to greet her.

'Mrs Elvin?' I said. 'I'm Veronica Guest and this is my husband. We live here just opposite you.'

She gave me a vivid smile. Something about her startled me. I very seldom use the word beautiful when describing anyone. I may say she or he is charming, attractive or good-looking, but I hardly ever use the word beautiful. It seems somehow too special. But there was no avoiding it now. There was no question about it, Nina Elvin was beautiful.

CHAPTER 2

Of course, I am not at all sure what I mean by beautiful.
It is not all a question of features. Nina Elvin had pleasant,
fine-boned features in an oval face. Her eyes were fine,
dark brown, large and set rather far apart. She had arched,
delicate eyebrows and a full-lipped mouth, and her hair,
which fell straight to her shoulders, was what I felt sure
was genuine blonde, contrasting strikingly with her dark
eyes. She was slender and gracefully built. But there was
something else about her that had very little to do with
these bare facts, a look of vitality, of strength of feeling,
of a gracious sort of friendliness, even while she was only
signing a receipt for the man who had brought her furniture, that impressed me instantly. At the same time, I felt
that there was something a little odd about her, but I think
there is always something odd about beauty. Perhaps it is
a touch of exaggeration, an air of somehow being a little
more in some respect than most people. At any rate, it
puts its possessor apart from most of us.

'I've heard of you from my brother Raymond,' she said.
She had the right voice to go with her looks, soft and rich.
'He said I'd find I was lucky in my neighbours.'

'That was nice of him,' I said. 'We're very good friends
with him and Marianne. But how are you managing?
Have you had any lunch? I could offer you a sandwich.'

'You're very kind,' she said, 'but I brought along some
frozen stuff and warmed it up in the microwave. We
haven't done so badly.'

I noticed that plural, so she was not alone.

'Is Raymond here with you now?' I asked.

'Yes, he's helping a great deal,' she said. 'What a job removing is, isn't it? I don't know where I'd have been without him. He's already managed to hang several of my pictures, while Marianne's been stacking my books in the bookshelves. There are some nice built-in bookshelves here, which saves me some bother. But may I ask you for something, as you've been so kind as actually to offer us lunch?'

Books, she had said. Were Nigel Elvin's books amongst them?

'Of course,' I said, 'and if we can help in any way, let us know.'

'Well, I'd give my soul for a cup of coffee –'

A fearful scream interrupted her. It came from inside the house, piercing and wild.

But it did not take the smile from her face.

'That child!' she exclaimed. 'I wonder what she's got up to. I think I'd better go and see.'

'I hope she hasn't hurt herself,' I said.

'Most unlikely,' her mother said. 'That isn't how she screams when she's hurt. It's one of her special screams when she's asserting herself.'

'Well, if you and the Markhams would like some coffee, come over as soon as you're ready,' I said.

'Thank you,' she said. 'Thank you so much.'

She turned towards the door, but did not seem in any great hurry. As she disappeared into the house, Alec and I turned towards our gate and made our way across our gravel courtyard to our own door.

'Didn't I say you'd be asking her in before you've had any time to get to know her?' Alec said.

'How am I to get to know her if I don't ask her in?' I inquired.

'The question is, is it necessary to get to know her at all?'

'Why shouldn't we? You aren't prejudiced against her because she's had a divorce, are you?'

'I'm not prejudiced against her in the least. I thought she seemed very attractive. But I don't see any need to be in such a hurry.'

'You just want to be awkward about it. Anyway, they probably won't stay long.'

He pushed open our door and we went into the house.

I went to the kitchen and plugged in the kettle, then put coffee-beans in the grinder and began to arrange cups and saucers on our tea-trolley. Our guests arrived about ten minutes later. Nina Elvin had a very small child by the hand. I am no good at guessing a child's age, but I put her at something between two and three. She was a pretty child, with her mother's blonde hair and large dark eyes which she fixed in a rather challenging way first on me, then on Alec.

Then she announced, 'Dada!'

We all laughed and Alec said, 'No such luck.'

'Really, Imogen,' Nina said, 'what mistakes will you make next?'

'Man,' Imogen stated.

'Ah, there you're absolutely right,' Raymond Markham said.

I knew that his age was thirty-five, because we had recently been to a birthday party given by the Markhams. He was about the same height as his sister, but heavily built and already putting on weight. A bulge inside his cardigan was beginning to become noticeable. Like her, he had an oval face which had some resemblance to hers yet could never have been called good-looking, though it had a friendly expression which was pleasant. He worked in an insurance firm in Gaysbrook.

Marianne was two or three years younger than he was.

She was small and slender, with a small face and small grey eyes and a small, rather tight-lipped mouth. She could not compare for looks with her sister-in-law, but in a neat, slightly pert way was quite attractive. She wore her brown hair cut very short, which drew attention to the fact that she was wearing long, brassy-looking earrings. She had on a long, full, brightly patterned skirt and a white shirt.

We settled down in the sitting-room and I brought the coffee in. Imogen, whose hand had been released by her mother, had followed me into the kitchen when I went to get the coffee and made a careful inspection of the room, opening any cupboard that was within her reach. Then she trotted into the dining-room, but came out in a moment and made for the stairs. She looked as if she was going to attempt to climb them, but at that point Nina emerged from the sitting-room and captured her, taking her back into the room with her and seating her firmly on her lap.

'You mustn't be a nuisance, darling,' Nina said. 'I hope you don't mind my having brought her, Mrs Guest. She'll settle down in a minute or two.'

'She's charming,' I answered. 'Are you thinking of sending her to school here? There's a school in the village – well, you can hardly call it a school, there are only about half a dozen children and it's run by a Miss Wiltman who's said to be a genius with the very young. It would be a way for her to meet other children.'

'That sounds like a very good idea,' Nina said, 'though I haven't thought much about things like that yet. What does one do – just get in touch with Miss Wiltman, or what?'

'I think so,' I said. 'She's in the phone book.'

'I'd go ahead with it, if I were you,' Raymond said. 'It'll get her off your hands for an hour or two.'

'Well, I must think about it,' Nina said. She caressed

29

the child's hair gently. As she had promised, Imogen seemed to be settling down, in fact, she looked like falling asleep on her mother's lap. Nina went on, 'Do you know what all that police activity was about this morning? I saw a car go by with its siren screaming.'

'Yes, one of our neighbours has had a burglary,' Alec answered. 'A very nasty affair. He's had an extremely valuable clock stolen.'

'A clock!' Raymond exclaimed. 'You aren't talking about Vic Ordway!'

'I'm afraid so – yes,' Alec said.

'Not the Tompion!'

'Yes.'

'Now that's really hard,' Raymond said. 'He was devoted to the thing. But I hadn't heard about the burglary. Do they think there's any chance of getting it back?'

'I think it's too early to say.'

'And it happened last night?'

'That's what the very little evidence they've got suggests. But Vic was in London for two nights, so I suppose it's just possible it happened on Thursday evening. Not that I see it makes much difference.'

'Anyway, I know it was insured,' Raymond said. 'Actually, with our people. D'you know who knew he was going to be away from home?'

'That's what he wants to know himself,' I said. 'It's making him suspicious of all his friends. We may all be under suspicion by now.'

'I don't believe that for a moment,' Marianne said. 'He's got too much sense. When he's got over the shock, he'll realize all kinds of people may have known he was away. Not that we've an alibi for either night. Have you?'

'No,' I said. 'Only what a husband and wife can give each other, and that doesn't count.'

She had strolled to the window and was standing there, looking out. Our sitting-room is a long room that goes from the front to the back of the house and has a window at each end. It was the front window at which she was standing, the one that overlooked Nina Elvin's bungalow. Suddenly, almost as if she were echoing me, though in a totally different tone, Marianne ejaculated, 'No!'

'What's the trouble?' Raymond asked.

'Nigel,' she answered. 'I swear it was Nigel. He got out of a car and went up to the door and rang the bell. Then he didn't wait, he just pushed it open and went in.'

'As a matter of fact,' Raymond said, 'we thought Nina was really shot of him.'

'We saw him this morning in the Green Man,' Alec said. 'We were with Vic Ordway.'

'You left your door unlocked?' I said. I was looking at Nina. She had not really stirred, but there was a rigidity about her that seemed new. Imogen, on her lap, appeared to have fallen asleep.

'No, as we were only coming across the way, it didn't seem worth bothering about,' Nina said. 'So you saw him this morning?'

'Yes,' Alec said.

'Did he say why he had come here?' Her voice was a little harsher than it had been a few minutes before.

'He said something about collecting some books that belong to him,' Alec answered.

'Books!' she said with contempt. 'I don't see Nigel going anywhere to collect books –'

'He's come out,' Marianne interrupted. 'He's got into his car and – yes, he's driving away.'

'I suppose that's because he didn't find me. Books – that's really comic!'

'I wonder if he's left some message there for you,' Raymond said. 'Perhaps I ought to go over and see. He may have tried to telephone you, then found that you weren't connected up yet.'

'Oh, don't bother,' Nina said. 'I know why he went in,

31

but he rather misjudged things. I'm sorry I wasn't there to tell him so.'

She had relaxed once more and was smiling in a way that gave a look of sarcastic amusement to her face. 'Settle down and enjoy Mrs Guest's delicious coffee.'

'You're thinking of your jewellery,' Raymond said.

'Of course. You see,' she went on, explaining to Alec and me, 'I've a certain amount of rather precious jewellery which I've always kept in the bank, but of course I've had to move it from London to Gaysbrook. It was given to me by my first husband. I sometimes used to wear some of it to please him while he was alive, but it was never really my sort of thing, and since he died I've never worn any of it except this ring.' She held out a hand. It was a long, slender, very elegant hand, worthy of the fine emerald and diamond ring that she wore on the fourth finger of her right hand. 'But Nigel wanted me to sell it all and I wouldn't. I haven't sold any of the things that Matthew gave me. That used to annoy Nigel, but specially he wanted the money for the jewellery, which he said it was sheer waste to leave in the bank. He used to say he wouldn't mind it if I'd wear it. But actually I believe he just wanted to get hold of some of it to give to his girl-friend, and I used to think that you never can tell, perhaps when Imogen's grown up she'll be the sort of girl who'll want to wear it. Anyway, it'll be up to her some day to decide whether she wants to keep it or sell it. Nigel isn't going to get it.'

'Suppose it really was the books that he was after,' I said.

She shook her head with a slight laugh. 'He could have had them for the asking.'

'But he said you never answered his letters when he did ask for them.'

'If they'd only been about his books I'd have done so. But they were obscene, horrible things. After I'd had one

32

or two, after he'd moved out of our flat, I didn't even read them. I kept them though, because I thought some day they might come in useful. If he started to make trouble about Imogen, for instance, wanting to see more of her than the weekends he's entitled to, or if he tried to turn her against me. They'd be pretty good evidence that he wasn't just the right sort of person to interfere in the bringing up of a young girl. But actually he hasn't made any trouble of that sort. He hasn't even bothered to try to see her. No, it's the jewellery he's after, not his books.'

'Where are you staying tonight?' I asked. 'In your house or with Raymond and Marianne?'

'Oh, in my house,' she answered. 'I've got our bedrooms and the kitchen fairly straight, so we can settle in quite easily. There's a charming little room for Imogen, opening out of mine, and she's fallen in love with it already. There's a dado of rabbits all round the walls and she's begun to give them names. I suppose it was a child's room before. I'm going to have most of the house redecorated, but that room can stay just as it is.'

The former owners had had no children, but perhaps they had hoped to have them and they simply had not come. That might be partly why they had felt the urge to move from the house and the neighbourhood in which they had suffered disappointment.

'We advised Nina to get all her decorating done before moving in,' Marianne said, 'but she was impatient to come.'

'I wanted to get away from that wretched flat in Fulham,' Nina said. 'I was happy there for about three months, and from then on only wanted to get away. But with Imogen coming and then to look after, going house-hunting wasn't too easy. Then Marianne wrote to tell me about this bungalow being on the market and I made a flying visit down here and snapped it up. It's just the kind of place we want, don't we, darling?' She dropped a light kiss on the sleeping Imogen's forehead. 'Now, I think we ought to go and get on with some work. It's been so nice of you to ask us in, Mrs Guest, and thank you so much for the coffee. It's put some energy back into me.'

She heaved the child up and planted her on her feet, then stood up herself. Imogen responded to this with a prodigious wail, which sounded to me much the same as the one that I had heard issue from the bungalow when we were first talking to her mother. Then she looked all round her, obviously puzzled as to how she had got where she was. Then she fixed a stare on Alec and, as she had before, announced, 'Dada!'

Alec laughed.

'My role seems to have been established,' he said.

'Of course, she wouldn't know her real father if she saw him,' Nina said. 'She's quite forgotten him. Children of that age forget so quickly. Now we really must go.'

She and the child and the Markhams trooped out of the house, with Alec following them and opening the gate for them. Coming back, he poured out for himself what was left of the coffee.

'Well, didn't I say you'd be having them in here sometime today?' he said.

'Only I think you said it would be for a cup of tea,' I said.

'Well, well, that I could be so wrong! What do you make of them?'

'I think I'll wait a little before I answer that. What did you think of them?'

'I like Imogen,' he said. 'That'll do to be going on with.'

The village stores stay open on a Saturday afternoon. Early closing day in Maddingleigh is Wednesday. When I had stacked the coffee cups in the dishwasher I took my shopping trolley and set off down to the village. Alec went into the garden and started hoeing a rose-bed. The stores are in a sort of small square at the heart of the village which is overlooked by the church, the school and the village hall, a building in which nearly all village activities are carried on. There is a small teashop, also the vicarage, and there are one or two private houses, in one of which the Markhams lived. I went into the stores and bought vegetables, cheese and some pâté, of which both Alec and I are particularly fond. As I left the stores a car stopped just outside it and the long, narrow form of Nigel Elvin slid out of it. He was not alone. A young girl was with him.

'Oh, hallo,' he said casually. 'Can I get cigarettes in here?'

'Yes,' I said. I had never bought any there myself, but I had seen them on a shelf above the counter.

The girl looked about twenty, was small and pretty in a pink and white childish way, had wavy brown hair, tied back from her face in a ponytail, wide blue eyes and a small, pouting mouth. She was wearing brilliantly patterned slacks and a yellow shirt.

'I won't be a minute,' Nigel Elvin said to her, going towards the door of the stores. Then he turned and came back. 'Sorry,' he said, 'I ought to introduce you. Karen Billson — Mrs Guest. Karen's my girlfriend, Mrs Guest. We live in Highgate. Nina can tell you all you may want to know about her. She made it her business to find out everything.'

His voice was bitter, but the girl gave a little giggle.

'Oh, Nigel, you shouldn't say that sort of thing. Not that it means anything much nowadays, does it, Mrs Guest? But I don't care much for having things advertised. Nigel and I are going to get married, now that the divorce is absolute at last.'

'We were just going into that place there for a cup of tea,' Nigel said. 'Would you join us?'

'I've just been drinking coffee,' I said. 'I don't think tea would go too well on top of it.'

'I dare say they could rise to giving you a coffee,' he said. 'Come with us, won't you? I'd be really grateful if you would. There are one or two things I think you could tell me.'

It was only curiosity that made me join them. I did not feel drawn to either of them and I did not want the coffee. But Nina Elvin had said enough about her former husband to make me think that it might be interesting to know some more about him.

I said, 'Thank you, but I mustn't stay for more than a very little while. I've some cooking to get on with at home.'

'Well, just wait a minute while I get some cigarettes.' He disappeared into the stores, re-emerging almost at once and leading the way over to the teashop.

It was very small, with frilly curtains at its windows, a display of home-made cakes on a counter that ran the length of it, four plastic-topped tables in a row and plastic chairs. There were small vases of flowers on all the tables. Mrs Cramer, who owned and ran the place, greeted me with, 'Hallo, Mrs Guest, nice to see you. It isn't often we *do* see you here.'

'Can you do us coffee?' Nigel asked, and when she said that certainly she could, he chose the table at which we were to sit and pulled a chair out for me. Then he opened his packet of cigarettes, held it out to me and when I shook my head, offered it to his girlfriend, who helped herself to one and waited for him to light it.

He had put a cigarette in his mouth and brought a lighter out of his pocket before it occurred to him to say to me, 'Mind if we do?'

I have become so unused to the people around me smoking that I felt a little bewildered, then shook my head once more and said, 'Well, what is it you want to know?'

'About Nina,' he said. 'D'you know if she's moving into that house today?'

'I think so,' I said.

'I went into it a little while ago,' he went on, 'thinking I might just catch her and be able to settle the matter of my books on the spot, but the place was empty. Yet the door wasn't locked.'

'Because she and the child and the Markhams were over with my husband and me,' I said. 'And she hadn't bothered to lock the door as we were only just across the way. Incidentally, Marianne saw you go in and come out of the bungalow.'

'My goodness!' Karen Billson said. 'I wouldn't leave our door unlocked even if I was only going across the road to the letter-box.'

'Because you don't live in a beautiful country village,' Nigel said, 'where they don't bother to steal anything smaller than grandfather clocks. About that clock, Mrs Guest, that old Vic had stolen, it's really valuable, is it?'

'I believe so,' I said. 'It's a Tompion, which means it dates from the seventeenth century, and this particular one is something special even as Tompions go. Losing it is just about breaking his heart. But perhaps I should tell you that Mrs Elvin appears to have no belief that it's your books that have brought you down here.'

'I know, I know, she thinks I'm after her jewellery. And I'll be honest with you, I wouldn't mind getting my hands on it. What's the point of keeping stuff that's just shut up in a bank? It would have been different if she'd sometimes worn it. But I'm not a thief, whatever she says of me. I sometimes steal other people's ideas when my own won't come, but I've never yet stolen even the smallest diamond.'

Karen gave another giggle. 'He's a journalist, you see. That's why he sometimes has to – well, let's say borrow other people's ideas.'

37

'That's absurd,' he said. 'If you borrow a thing you have to give it back, and how can you give back an idea once you've helped yourself to it? No, if I need an idea, I just go ahead and steal it.'

'You know Vic fairly well, don't you?' I said. 'How long have you known him?'

'About a couple of years, I suppose it is. I once decided to do a series on antiques for the *Morning Herald*, and as I'm quite ignorant on the subject, it meant interviewing a number of dealers in different parts of the country. Vic was one of the people I saw and he was very helpful. It was a queer thing, we began by getting along extraordinarily well together, then something changed and he made it plain he'd no use for me. I've always assumed it was Nina who put him off. I can't be sure of it, but I think that once he discovered I'd a connection with her and the Markhams, and of course heard her version of what had gone wrong in our relationship, he wanted to have as little to do with me as possible.'

'But didn't he show you the Tompion?'

He shook his head, tipping some ash from his cigarette into the ashtray on the table.

'Not that I remember.'

'Oh, I'm sure you'd have remembered it if he ever had.'

He gave a smile. It was crooked and sarcastic. 'It wouldn't have meant very much to me. I told you I was quite ignorant on the subject.'

'I see,' I said. 'But of course you came to Maddingleigh with your wife to visit the Markhams before the troubles started between you.'

'As a matter of fact, no,' he said. 'Ray and Marianne came to visit us in London, but today is the first time I've come here.'

'This morning you seemed extraordinarily interested in where Vic had stayed when he was in London. Was there any reason for that?'

38

'Suppose there was?'

'Oh, I know it's not my business. It just seemed a bit odd, that's all. Now I really must be going. Thank you for my coffee.'

They both stood up as I got to my feet and dragged my trolley out into the road.

I walked home slowly, wondering why I felt that I had missed something of interest in that brief conversation, something that related to what had happened in the village that day. Was it the fact that the man had not asked a single question about Imogen? No, that was not really so remarkable, his circumstances being what they were. It was something more elusive. Then suddenly I realized what it was, and it really did not seem important. It was simply that Nigel Elvin had invited me to join him and Karen for a cup of tea because there were one or two things that he thought I could tell him. He had said that he would be really grateful if I would do this. But in the event it had been I who had asked him questions which he had answered readily enough. Had he in fact asked me anything? Yes, he had asked me if Nina Elvin was moving into her house that day. But that was about all. The fact was, I thought, simply that it had struck him that it might be useful to cultivate me as a link with Nina in case this should be needed. I might perhaps persuade her to part with those books of his, if he, rather than she, was to be believed about them.

When I arrived home I went into the kitchen to start cooking our evening meal. I had intended to make a goulash, but I was feeling very tired and it seemed rather too demanding. I took some frozen duck in orange sauce out of the freezer, switched on the oven, and while it heated sliced up some runner beans that Alec had brought in from the garden and finished peeling the potatoes that I had begun in the morning. Then, presently, when the duck was in the oven and the beans and potatoes were simmering on the stove, I went into the sitting-room, dropped into a chair and demanded sherry.

Alec was on the sofa, reading a Rex Stout. He got up, went to our drinks cupboard and poured out sherry for us both. I told him about my meeting with Nigel Elvin and Karen Billson and as much as I could remember of our conversation, and he listened without seeming too interested until after a time he said, 'This girl – Karen – she was in the car with him when you met him.'

'Yes,' I said.

'I wonder how she got there.'

'How do you mean?'

He had sat down on the sofa again, put up his feet and sipped some sherry.

'Do you think she was in the car outside when he came into the Green Man this morning?' he asked. 'And if so, why did he leave her there instead of bringing her in with him?'

'I don't know. I hadn't thought about it,' I said.

'Do you think he left her there so that she shouldn't have to face Vic, or whoever else might be there, after all the clamour there was about the divorce?'

'I can't really see either of them being so delicate in their feelings.'

'Or do you think she just doesn't like pubs?'

'I can't quite see that either.'

'Well, if she wasn't waiting for him in the car, where was she?'

'Does it matter?'

'Probably not.'

'Perhaps she only came down to Gaysbrook this afternoon, and when I met them he'd just been into the station there to pick her up.'

'Only it would mean either that he'd arranged with her that she was to do that before he came down here, or that

40

he'd send for her, wouldn't it? And why should they have done either of those things?'

'Yes, indeed, why?'

He gave a sigh. 'Let's talk about something else. Poor Vic and his burglary are really nothing to do with us, and we can't do anything to help. And I'm beginning to think we made a mistake laying out such a big patch of the garden for vegetables. We always waste half of them. What about reducing the size of it and making a pergola that reaches to a small water garden at the end? We could have some goldfish in the pool, and of course lilies . . .'

We went on to talk of the changes we might make in the garden, a thing we often do, though somehow we do not get around to making the changes. Then suddenly we were interrupted by the ringing of our doorbell.

I went to answer it. It was Vic who stood on our doorstep. His small monkey face looked drawn and tired.

'May I come in?' he said. 'If you've had enough of me and my problems today, just say so, but I'd be very grateful for some quiet company and a little civilized conversation.'

I put out a hand and drew him indoors.

'Have you still got the police with you?' I asked as I closed the door behind him.

'No, thank God they've gone, at least for the moment,' he said. 'I expect they'll be back tomorrow. And I suppose I shouldn't complain if they're being thorough, but I feel quite worn out. I must have told my story to them, I mean of why I went to London and came home this morning and found my poor old Tompion gone, at least half a dozen times. They've been trying hard to find out who might have known I was going to be away, badgering poor Giles in the shop, because of course he knew about my going, and so on. I've never thought much about what it means to be burgled, but I can tell you this, I don't recommend it.'

We were in the sitting-room by then and Alec had stood

41

up and without asking Vic what he wanted, was pouring him out a stiff whisky. He accepted it with an appreciative little smile, and sank down into one of our easy chairs, letting out a long breath.

'Now if you want to be really good to me,' he said, after he'd taken a gulp of his drink, 'will Alec please play something for me. Anything as long as it's quiet and soothing.'

Alec, perhaps I should mention, is a moderately talented pianist. He plays solely for his own pleasure and can very seldom be persuaded to play for anyone else. I am so entirely unmusical myself that I do not know how to rate his ability, but I am inclined to think that it is slightly more than he himself believes. I did not expect him to respond to Vic's request, but I suppose because he was sorry for him, he sat down and started to play. I think it was Chopin. Vic stretched out comfortably in his chair and closed his eyes, opening them only when he wanted to sip at his drink, and when presently Alec stood up and returned to his sherry, said, 'Thank you, Alec, that was really good of you. If there were more people like you and Veronica around, perhaps I shouldn't be thinking of going away.'

'Going away!' I exclaimed. 'You aren't serious.'

'I don't know how serious I'll be about it tomorrow,' he said, 'but this evening I'm very serious indeed.'

Alec smiled. 'We'll wait for tomorrow.'

'No, but really . . .' Vic's face was certainly serious. 'I haven't been talking about it, but I've been thinking about it for some time. Things haven't been going well for me. The shop's been pretty much of a dead loss recently. People haven't got the money. So I've been thinking of selling up and starting some sort of a new life somewhere. Not in antiques. I've got enough put by to live fairly comfortably without a job for quite a while.'

42

'But in that case, why move away?' Alec asked. 'Haven't you been happy here?'

'Oh, very, very. That's partly why I feel I've got to go. It would be so different here once I'd given up the shop. I think I'd age ten years overnight.'

'Have you given any thought yet to where you'd like to go?'

'I've been thinking of Australia. Adelaide. I've been told by an Australian friend that once you've lived in Adelaide you'll never want to live anywhere else.'

'How many other places have you thought of going to in your time?'

'Oh, I know you think I'm talking nonsense, and I probably am. I dare say it will all seem different tomorrow. All the same, I've been really attracted for some time by the thought of moving a long way away, and this beastly affair today has made me want to get ahead with it.'

'Well, I can understand that,' Alec said, 'but you'll get over it.'

'At the moment I don't even want to get over it.'

'By the way,' I said, 'I met your friend Nigel Elvin in the village and had coffee with him and his girlfriend, Karen Billson. Do you know her?'

Vic shook his head without much show of interest.

'I don't much like his hanging around the place at the moment,' he said. 'The Markhams have told me Nina wants to be free of him. I don't know anything about his girlfriend, except that she's one amongst many. Now I must be going. And thank you for the drink and the Chopin. Wherever I end up, you must certainly come and visit me.'

He finished his drink and Alec went with him down to the gate. I was relieved that he had not stayed any longer, for if he had we should certainly have had to ask him to stay to dinner, and I had put only two portions of duck in the oven.

I served them up presently, after we had had second drinks, then we had biscuits and cheese. Because we were both tired we went to bed early, as soon as we had listened to the nine o'clock news, and I fell asleep almost at once.

I woke early too, or what is early for me. It was just seven o'clock when I opened my eyes and looked at the clock.

It was five minutes later that the screaming started.

CHAPTER 3

My first thought was of the child's scream in the bungalow.

Then I realized that it was not a child's scream. It was an adult who was making that fearful noise, in which it seemed to me I could distinguish the word, 'Help!'

Alec was still asleep. I put a hand on his shoulder and shook him. He woke drowsily, but then suddenly sat upright in the bed, staring at the window through which the sounds were reaching us. Then he scrambled out of bed, pulled on trousers and pullover over his pyjamas, and made for the door. I snatched up my dressing-gown, slid my feet into my slippers, and followed him. The screaming had stopped for a moment, but then began again, sounding even louder and more desperate than before. Alec flung open our front door and ran across our courtyard to the gate. With my dressing-gown flapping around me, I followed him. The morning was clear and mild. The sky was a pale blue, with not a cloud to be seen.

As soon as Alec reached the gate, the screaming stopped. He shot across the road and I followed him as quickly as I could. Nina Elvin was standing in the carport, beside a car which was not her Mercedes. She was wearing a nightdress, her hair was dishevelled and her feet were bare. Her hands clasped each side of her head. As soon as Alec reached her side she began to sob, and, dropping her hands and pointing, cried out, 'Look, look!'

What she was pointing at was something that lay at her

feet. It was the long, very thin body of a man, and it took me only a moment to recognize Nigel Elvin. He was on his side, with his arms and legs sprawled out, and something sticking out of his back. It looked as if it might be a knife and there was a puddle of blood around it. It was dry-looking blood. If he had been stabbed to death, it must have happened some hours ago.

Nina caught hold of Alec's arm and clung to him.

'Thank God you heard me!' she sobbed. 'I didn't know what to do. It's Nigel. He's dead. And I couldn't leave Imogen alone in the house and the phone isn't connected, so I didn't know how to get in touch with anyone, so I tried calling out, hoping you'd hear me. Oh, I'm so thankful you did! Now you can phone the police for me. But wait a moment while I get into my dressing-gown. Just stay here and make sure no one comes by. There's been no one since I came out and found him, but someone might come along at any moment – you never know. So wait here and I won't be a minute.'

She turned and fled into the house.

Alec looked at me and said, 'Hadn't you better get dressed?'

'Presently,' I said. I was speaking with a strange, internal sort of tremor. I had not seen many dead people, and those whom I had seen had been serenely dead in bed. I had not been frightened by the sight of them. But the sight of this murdered man, with the knife in his back, filled me with terror. He must have fallen where he had been standing when he was stabbed. I noticed something bright on the ground near one of his outflung hands and realized that it was a car-key. So he had been about to get into his car when he had been attacked. I recognized the car. It was the one that Nigel Elvin had been driving when I met him and Karen Billson in the village.

Alec and I were silent as we waited for Nina to reappear. When she did she was not in a dressing-gown but had put on jeans, a sweater and sandals and was carrying her shoulder-bag. She had even given herself the time to pull a comb through her hair. But her face was of a sickly pallor, with lines etched deeply into it where yesterday there had been no lines at all.

'You'll telephone the police for me, won't you?' she said to Alec.

'Wouldn't it be better if you did that yourself?' he said.

'But I can't leave Imogen,' she said.

'Anyway, tell us just what happened. How did you find out about it?'

'I saw it from the bathroom window.' She turned and pointed at a window that overlooked the carport. 'I went in there for a shower and first saw the car that had no right to be there and then – then I saw *him* . . . Not that I knew at first glance who it was, but then I suddenly realized, and I felt – I felt absolutely terrified. I suppose I'd have felt much the same whoever it was, but recognizing Nigel – I mean, they're going to think I did it, aren't they? I hated him. I hated him for several years. He was cruel to me. He tortured me. But I didn't do it. I wouldn't do it to anyone.'

'It must have happened quite a time ago,' Alec said. 'That blood's about dry. Did you hear nothing in the night? Nothing suspicious?'

'No. I slept like the dead. Oh dear, I shouldn't have said that. He doesn't look as if he's asleep, does he? But I was deadly tired after all the work in the house yesterday. And I don't often get up as early as this, but I wanted to get working again. Then I didn't know what to do about getting hold of the police, so I tried screaming. And it worked. You heard me. God be thanked!'

'Well, I think the best thing for us to do now,' I said, 'is for you to get Imogen and come over to the house with me and, as Alec suggested, phone the police yourself, while he stays here and keeps a watch on things. Shall we do that?'

She looked doubtful. 'I suppose it's the right thing to do. Only the thought of phoning them and telling them . . . all right, I'll do it. Wait for me while I get Imogen up.'

She disappeared into the bungalow again.

When she had gone, Alec said thoughtfully, 'Did she do it?'

'Whatever makes you say that?' I asked.

'Well, did she?'

'She'd no reason to, had she?' I said. 'She'd got her divorce. She'd got rid of him. And I believe she's got plenty of money. She hasn't got to try to get it out of him.'

'But what was he doing here? He came here for a reason, didn't he?'

'D'you mean you think he'd some hold over her, and perhaps was going to try to blackmail her, or something?'

'It isn't impossible, but I hadn't thought of anything as specific as that.'

'I wonder what's happened to his girlfriend?'

'The police are going to look into that, I suppose.'

'I wonder if she stayed at the Green Man, or went back to London.'

While we were talking, I had been edging further and further away from that terrible thing on the ground, and Alec had been staying beside me. By the time that Nina came out of the house, holding Imogen by the hand, we could still see it, but felt a little detached from it, which was calming to the nerves. But when Nina came out of the front door, Imogen was crying and her high, shrill wailing started that internal trembling in me again, so that I thought that the quicker we could reach our house, the better it would be.

But Imogen did not want to go. She did her best to hold back, and shrieked, 'No, no – don't want!'

It was not that she had seen what was in the carport,

48

or even if she had that she would have known what it meant, but plainly she resented deeply being hauled out of bed at an unfamiliar hour to be taken she did not know where.

'I'll stay here until the police arrive,' Alec said to Nina. 'They won't be long.'

'Thank you,' Nina said. 'You're both being very kind to me. Come along, Imogen. Don't make such a fuss.'

'Don't want!' the child wailed.

'I'm sorry about this,' Nina said. 'She knows something's wrong and she's frightened, but she'll calm down once we get her away.'

At that moment Imogen caught sight of Alec, and pointing at him, shouted, 'Dada!'

'Oh, come along,' Nina said, and started towards our gate, giving Imogen a sharp pull beside her.

I went in with them at our gate and then led the way up to our door, which we had left standing open.

We went into the sitting-room and Nina dropped abruptly into a chair as if her strength had suddenly deserted her. She leant her head back and closed her eyes. This seemed to bewilder Imogen, who became wonderingly silent, standing staring up at her mother with her eyes very wide open and her mouth open too. As her mother remained rigid and silent, she put out a hand and plucked furtively at Nina's jeans.

'I'll make some tea,' I said. 'I'll do it while you're phoning.'

'Phoning?' Nina said vaguely, opening her eyes and looking round her as if she had forgotten where she was. 'Oh yes, phoning . . . Have you got their number?'

'It'll be in the book,' I said. 'I've never had occasion to phone the police, so we haven't a note of it.'

'The Gaysbrook people, I suppose.'

The phone book was on a shelf under the table on which the telephone stood, and Nina picked it up and started

49

turning the pages, but after a moment put it down and said, 'I'm being stupid. We dial 999, don't we?'

She was about to pick up the telephone when Imogen snatched it up, clapped it to her ear and screamed, ' 'lo, 'lo, 'lo!'

'Oh, darling, do keep quiet for just a few minutes, can't you?' Nina said in an exhausted voice, took the telephone from the child and began to dial. But suddenly she slammed it down and took a quick step back from it. 'Oh, Veronica, I can't – I just can't do it! Won't you do it for me? You know all there is to tell them. Please do it – please!'

'I really think you ought to do it,' I said.

'But I can't, I really can't! My voice will go, I'll get muddled, I'll get everything wrong. Oh, I'm so frightened of doing it. Won't you do it – please?'

It was difficult to resist such imploring. I picked up the telephone and dialled. I had no idea what I was going to say and suddenly felt a fear of what I had to do which made me more sympathetic to Nina than I had been when she first asked me to do her telephoning for her. Once I was through to someone who said he was the police in Gaysbrook, I asked for Inspector Frayne. But I was told that he was not in his office, and the voice did not sound particularly interested. It asked if I could give some indication of what I wanted him for.

'I want to report a murder,' I said.

'Yes? A murder? Where would that be?'

'In a bungalow in the village of Maddingleigh. A man called Nigel Elvin has been stabbed in the back in the carport. The body was discovered about half an hour ago by his wife – his ex-wife – they're divorced. She only moved into the bungalow yesterday and her telephone isn't connected, so I'm phoning for her. My name's Veronica Guest and I live in the house opposite to the bungalow. It's called Lychwood.'

'And you're sure he's dead, this man?' the voice said.

'Absolutely sure.'

'What was he doing there if he was divorced from his wife?'

'I assume that's for you to find out. This isn't a hoax call.'

There was another silence, a longer one; in fact, I began to wonder if I had been cut off. Then a different voice spoke. It had a certain sound of authority in it.

'Mrs Guest?'

'Yes.'

'You'll be there when we arrive shortly?'

'Yes.'

'Very well. You're in your own house, are you, not in the bungalow?'

'Yes, but my husband's over there, keeping a watch on things.'

'Good. Well, we'll be along as quickly as we're able. Where's Mrs Elvin?'

'In here with me, too shocked to be able to make this call.'

'I see. Thank you.'

The line went dead. I put down our telephone and turned to Nina. She had Imogen on her lap and was murmuring something to her which for the moment was keeping her quiet, though tears were rolling down her cheeks.

'Has she had any breakfast yet?' I asked.

'No, and I think that's what's the trouble with her,' Nina answered.

'What does she usually have for breakfast?'

'Oh, just some milk and some cereal.'

'Well, I can manage that. And I can make some tea for you and me. Let's go into the kitchen.'

She set Imogen down on her feet, took her hand and led her after me into the kitchen.

I put a packet of cornflakes, a bottle of milk and a dish

51

on the table, and left it to Nina to serve Imogen with what she would want, while I filled the kettle and fetched the teapot and cups and saucers out of a cupboard.

At first we were silent, then Nina said, 'I haven't thanked you for making that call. It was very good of you.'

'I don't think they wanted to believe me,' I said. 'I didn't really know how to put it.'

'I suppose they do get hoax calls, or perhaps calls from people who are just hysterical and upset and think some minor accident's a murder.' Nina sounded more composed now, though her face still had the pallor that put ten years on her age. But I could see again the beauty that had struck me so startlingly when I saw her first.

'Did Nigel come to see you yesterday?' I asked.

'Oh, no.'

'Then what were he and his car doing in the carport?'

She did not answer at once, but gazed straight before her with a vague, unfocused stare. Then after a moment she said, 'I wish I didn't know.'

'You do know, do you?'

'I nearly always knew what Nigel was doing and why. That was one of the reasons why things were so difficult. He couldn't bear it that I should know so much about him.'

'What was there so awful about him that he should mind so much if you knew it?'

'Well, I always knew it when he had a new woman in tow, and when he'd got some scheme going with some of his more awful friends. That used to frighten me and I'd try pretty desperately to make him give it up, and that used to enrage him and he'd generally knock me about.'

'Are you saying that he was some kind of a crook?'

'Of course.'

'But what brought him to your new house?'

'Not love of me.'

'All right, you don't want to tell me,' I said, 'and it isn't any business of mine, but the police won't let you off so easily. I'd advise you to stick to it that you know nothing about it, or else be prepared to tell them all you know.'

'But they're going to suspect me anyhow, aren't they?'

'You'll be one of the people under suspicion. But remember that something rather peculiar happened here yesterday, or rather, the night before last. A very valuable clock was stolen. If your husband was the crook you say he was, his being down here might be connected with that. Not that it explains what he was doing in your car-port a whole day after the theft, but it's somehow a bit much of a coincidence that two major crimes should have happened so close together in a quiet spot like this.'

She wrinkled her brow, looking puzzled. Imogen was busily spooning up her cornflakes and drinking her milk and paying no attention to either of us.

'You mean that he might have known something about that theft, and been killed because he was a danger to someone?' Nina said. She sounded hopeful, as if she liked the idea.

'It's a possibility, isn't it, if he was really the kind of person you say?'

'But it isn't the only possibility.' She reached out a hand for her shoulder-bag that she had been wearing and had deposited on a chair, opened it and turned it upside down over the table.

A cascade of glittering objects fell out of the bag. I gasped. I know next to nothing about jewellery, but that these were diamonds, rubies, emeralds and pearls seemed absolutely certain to me. There were necklaces, bracelets, earrings and brooches. If the gems were genuine, the heap on the table must represent a great deal of money. I moved back from them, as if they were some kind of threat to me.

'You see,' she said.

'You've had them with you all this time?' I stammered.

'Yes, I'd have put them in the bank in Gaysbrook where I opened an account last week, but it was Saturday, and they're one of the banks that don't open at all on a Saturday. So I had to bring them with me and they've been on my mind ever since.'

'And you think your husband knew you'd got them all there in the bungalow?'

'I think he must have done.'

'But how?'

She did not answer at once, but added some milk to the remaining cornflakes in Imogen's bowl.

'How?' I repeated.

'Perhaps he didn't really,' she said. 'It's just an idea of mine that somehow he got to know I'd got the jewels and came to rob me. One way he might have done it is simply by remembering that the bank where I always kept the jewels in Fulham didn't open on a Saturday, and assuming that I'd have my account transferred to a branch of the same bank in Gaysbrook, guessed that one of the first things I'd do when I got here was deposit the jewels with them. And he'd know that the day was Saturday and that I wouldn't actually be able to do that.'

'But that would mean that he'd been keeping an eye on you. He'd have had to do that to know that you'd got the jewellery from the Fulham branch and that you came down to stay with the Markhams on Friday, too late to go to the bank. Do you think he'd been doing that?'

'I wouldn't put it past him.'

'With what object?'

'To make me suffer in some way.'

'Of course, if he did know you had the jewels...' I paused.

'Yes?'

'It's just that he might have let the information on to someone else, and they planned the robbery together, then something went wrong, they fell out and there was a murder.'

'Murder,' Imogen said thoughtfully, pleased with herself for having acquired a new word.

The doorbell rang.

Nina swept all the jewellery back into the shoulder-bag and slung it on her shoulder.

I went to open the door and found two tall men who could only be policemen on the doorstep.

One of them introduced himself and his companion. 'Detective Superintendent Berry, and this is Detective Sergeant Quarles. Mrs Elvin?'

'No, I'm Mrs Guest,' I said. 'Mrs Elvin is in here. Come in.'

'It was you who telephoned, then,' the superintendent said.

'Yes, Mrs Elvin wasn't in a state to be able to do it.'

I took the two men into the sitting-room. The superintendent was a burly man, probably in his forties, with a broad, bland face with slightly bulging grey eyes, a little nose and a broad but thin-lipped mouth. The sergeant looked about ten years younger, and had shaggy fair hair, intent blue eyes and a long, narrow face.

'We've just been down to the bungalow and talked to your husband, Mrs Guest,' the superintendent went on. 'He told us it was Mrs Elvin who discovered the body and that we should find her here.'

'I'll fetch her,' I said, and went out to the kitchen.

I did not know in what state Nina would be when she had to face the police and I had the feeling when I saw her that she had not quite made up her own mind about this. Should she be shattered and hysterical or icily, absolutely calm? It was only for a moment that I felt this doubt, a sense that it was in her power to choose what role it would be best for her to play, because almost at once it seemed to me that she was too frightened to adopt any pose deliberately.

Taking Imogen by the hand, she went to the sitting-room and said, 'I'm sorry to keep you. I'm Nina Elvin.'

Imogen stood still in the doorway, pulling against her mother's hand, and stared at the men, then decided to give a loud wail.

'Now for heaven's sake, be quiet,' Nina said impatiently. 'You've seen strange men before. I'm sorry if she's diffi-cult, Superintendent, but of course I can't leave her alone, and she's puzzled and upset about everything already.'

'Quite understandable,' the superintendent said. 'What's your name, little girl?'

This was one of the few questions that Imogen under-stood, and she answered, 'Mo.'

'It's Imogen,' Nina said, 'and she can say it quite prop-erly when she's in the mood.'

'What a pretty name,' he said, trying to placate the child.

'Won't you sit down?' I said. 'Or do you want Mrs Elvin to go over to the bungalow?'

'Not just at the moment,' he said, looking round for a chair. 'There are a few things we can go into quickly while we're here. Then we'll see.'

We all sat down, Imogen climbing on to Nina's lap, but keeping her gaze fixedly on the two men.

'Now, I believe you've identified the dead man as your husband, Nigel Elvin, whom you've recently divorced,' the superintendent went on. 'Can you tell us when you last saw him?'

'Alive?'

'Yes, alive.'

'No, I don't think I can. It's some months ago, anyway.'

'You didn't see him on his visit here, then?'

'No.'

'He didn't call on you?'

'No.'

56

'Do you know why he came here?'

She hesitated very briefly, and I thought of what was in the shoulder-bag that she was wearing and wondered if she meant to tell the men what she had told me about it in the kitchen. But after only an instant of uncertainty she said, 'I believe it was about some books.'

'Books?' he said.

'Yes, he claimed I'd some books that were unpacked yesterday and some of them may have been his. He wrote to me about them several times, and said that if I didn't send them to him he'd come and get them, but I couldn't send them because I'd lost my record of which they were. So perhaps that's why he came, but I'm only guessing.'

She was putting a lot of trust in me, I thought, assuming that I would not simply tell the detectives about the jewellery. For the moment, at least, I was silent, though I did not understand why she should want to keep the truth about it to herself. Perhaps she did not fully understand it herself, I thought. There was something rather mysterious about that jewellery. Suddenly I wondered if it was all genuine, or if some of it at least could be fake. But if it was it would hardly have brought Nigel Elvin all the way here to commit a burglary.

'Now, it was you who discovered the body, Mrs Elvin, so Mr Guest has told us,' Berry went on. 'Will you tell us how that happened?'

She told him how she had seen the body from the bathroom window, telling it in almost the same words as she had used when she told it to Alec and me.

'And this was at about seven o'clock,' he said.

'I suppose so. I didn't really notice the time,' she replied.

'But Dr Daly says he must have been killed before midnight. That's only a rough estimate, of course, and it will have to be confirmed, but it seems certain that he'd been lying where you found him for some hours. Now we must go. We'll be wanting to see you again presently. You'll be here, will you?'

Nina gave me a quick, questioning look, and I answered the question, 'Of course.'

The two men stood up and I led the way to the front door and let them out.

As soon as I returned to the sitting-room, I exclaimed, 'Now why on earth did you do that, Nina? I mean about the jewellery. Saying nothing about it. Why were you afraid of letting them know you'd got it here?'

She gave me a confused, vacant look.

'You think that was a mistake?'

'Of course it was. You'll have to tell them about it sooner or later, and they'll wonder why you didn't tell them about it before.'

'Yes, I see. Well, I don't know why I didn't do it. I'm so muddled and lost, Veronica, I hardly know anything about what I'm doing. Yes, of course I ought to have told them. It was very stupid of me not to. D'you think I should go after them now and tell them?'

'They told you to stay here,' I said. 'I should wait until they come back.'

'There's another thing I didn't tell them,' she said, 'because I didn't really understand what they were asking until just before they went. They asked when I last saw Nigel and I said it was months ago. But actually I saw him last night.'

I gave a snort of exasperation. 'If that's true, why ever didn't you say so?'

'Because when they asked me the question I thought they meant when had I actually met him and talked to him face to face. And that was months ago. But I did catch sight of him passing the house about ten o'clock, I think it was. I just had a glimpse of him, going by with another man. I didn't think very much about it at the time. I knew that he was in Maddingleigh, because Marianne had seen

58

him go in and out of the house, d'you remember, and then I heard about you and Alec meeting him in the Green Man, but I didn't think it could be anything very important. Perhaps, I thought, it might really be about those books of his. So I told those policemen about the books, because I knew at least, after all his letters, that he wanted them.'

'You say you saw him go by with another man,' I said. 'What was the man like?'

But before she could answer that our front door was opened and Alec came in. He looked very tired, as he might have looked if he had been up all night instead of sleeping soundly until our gruesome waking. Murder had taken it out of him. He was a sensitive man and keeping watch over a corpse was not the sort of occupation that suited him. He dropped into a chair and as soon as he had done that Imogen left her mother and climbed up on to his lap.

'Dada,' she said lovingly, and gave him a little kiss on one cheek.

I thought for a moment that he was going to push her away, he looked so nervous and irritable, but if he had had that impulse he controlled it, and gently stroked her hair.

'What about breakfast?' he said to me. 'Have you had it?'

'Imogen's had it,' I said, 'but Nina and I have just had some tea. I'll get us some breakfast now. And while I'm doing it . . .' I turned to Nina. 'You could tell Alec about the jewellery.'

'Jewellery?' Alec said.

Nina gave me a look that was far from friendly.

'I think I was stupid to show it to you,' she said. 'It probably isn't in the least important, but you're really doing your best to make it seem as if it's at the heart of the case. However, of course I'll show it to Alec.'

She slipped her bag off her shoulder, opened it and turned it upside down over the coffee-table. The gleaming jewels tumbled out on to it. Alec drew his breath in sharply, then firmly moved Imogen off his lap, stood up and crossed to the table.

Imogen followed him and, as he stood looking down at the heap, made a grab at a diamond earring, held it up and exclaimed, 'Pretty!'

'Are they genuine?' Alec asked.

'To the best of my knowledge,' Nina replied.

'What are they doing here?'

'Go on, tell him,' I said, 'while I'm getting the breakfast.'

But I stayed in the room just long enough to make sure that she was going to tell him the same story about the jewellery and how it came to be here as she had told me. It was curious to realize that I had begun to feel a distrust of her for which I could not really account. Naturally, it had something to do with her failure to tell the police the truth about the jewellery, yet on meeting her I had taken a warm liking to her and I still felt this as much as ever. The distrust was somehow confused with pity. I felt that she was floundering in waters that were much too deep for her, oppressed by a frightening ignorance of how to strike out for safety.

I made coffee, poured cornflakes into three bowls and called out that breakfast was ready.

They came into the kitchen and sat down round the table. From the fact that Nina had her bag swung on her shoulder again, I deduced that the jewels were back inside it.

Pouring out coffee, I said to her, 'You were just going to tell me about seeing Nigel go past the house with another man, but Alec came in and interrupted you. Alec, the police asked Nina when she saw Nigel last and she said it was months ago, but after they'd gone she told me

60

that she saw him last night around ten o'clock. What was that other man like, Nina?'

'I didn't really notice,' she said. 'It was fairly dark.'

'Have you even a rough idea of him?'

'Well, he was short and thin and had fair hair and glasses. I can't remember what he was wearing.'

I looked questioningly at Alec. He shook his head.

'Conveys nothing to me, unless possibly . . .' He paused. 'But no, Giles isn't short.'

'It could be hundreds of other people too,' I said. 'I wonder what's happened to Karen Billson. Even if she spent the night here, it's possible she doesn't know what's become of Nigel. If they had separate rooms in the Green Man she may simply be wondering where on earth he's gone.'

'She'd have gone to look in his room, wouldn't she, and she'd see that his bed hadn't been slept in,' Alec said. 'You know, I think we ought to try phoning to see if she does know what's happened.'

'Karen Billson?' Nina said. 'Who's she?'

Alec and I exchanged glances. He plainly wanted to leave it to me to tell her about Karen, and this really made sense, since it was I who had seen her.

'She's a girlfriend of Nigel's, who's down here at the moment,' I said. 'I think she came down to Gaysbrook in the afternoon. Anyway, I ran into the two of them together in the village yesterday, and I think they were going to be spending the night at the Green Man.'

'Poor girl,' Nina said.

'You don't think he'd have stuck to her?' I said.

'Better for her if he didn't. He never treated any of his women decently. But you aren't going to phone her, are you?'

'Why not?' Alec said.

'Just phone her? "Hallo, hallo, your boyfriend's dead, did you know?"' Nina shook her head vigorously. 'No,

61

you can't possibly do that, it would be too cruel. It would be kinder to tell that detective about her and have him send one of his men to break the news to her. You ought to have told him to do that. You ought to have told him about her, of course, Veronica. That's another thing we've got wrong between us. But that reminds me, may I use your phone to ring Raymond and tell him what's happened? I don't know why I didn't think of doing that sooner. You know he and Marianne were with me for supper yesterday evening. I wish they'd stayed later than they did. It might have been a help now.'

'Go ahead,' Alec said, and she got up and went back to the sitting-room, where our telephone is. We heard the tinkle it gives when it is picked up and then, only a moment afterwards, our doorbell rang.

Alec went to answer it and brought Detective Sergeant Quarles into the kitchen.

'Sorry to trouble you again so soon,' he said, 'but there was something we ought to have asked you when we were here before.'

'Would you like some coffee?' I asked.

'Now that would be really nice,' he answered. 'But let me just ask you this question first. Does Garnish's Hotel, Bolt Street, mean anything to you?'

It did. I knew at once that I had heard of it, but I could not think where. Then suddenly the memory came. But Alec's had come a little faster than mine.

'Yes, we heard Nigel Elvin speak of it to Victor Ordway yesterday morning. I think Ordway had stayed there when he was in London, the night his clock was stolen and the night before. I don't know how Elvin knew of it. Why?'

The sergeant had accepted the cup of coffee that I handed him.

'It's merely that there's a note of it on an envelope in Elvin's pocket. May mean nothing, may be important. What you've just said about it makes me feel it might be important. The theft of the clock, Elvin knowing where Ordway would be for those two nights, and then the murder . . .'

The doorbell rang again.

I went to answer it this time. It was Karen Billson on the doorstep.

CHAPTER 4

The pink and white prettiness of the day before had gone. Her face was grey. Her hair was unkempt. With one hand she was clutching a doorpost, as if she were afraid of falling over.

'I'm sorry . . . I didn't know . . . I don't know what . . .' The words came tumbling out almost unintelligibly. She took a deep breath and began again. 'I'm sorry to trouble you, but they sent me here. That detective over there. He told me to come here and wait for him.'

'That's all right – come in,' I said.

She staggered in at the door. I took her by the elbow and guided her towards the kitchen. I could feel her trembling.

'How did you hear about it?' I asked.

'One of the waiters at the Green Man told me,' she answered. 'He'd heard about it from the milkman and he told me about it when I came down to breakfast. I came straight down here and asked that policeman there what had really happened. He told me . . . He said . . .' She began to lose control of herself again, but pulled herself rigidly together. 'Well, he told me Nigel was dead, and it was murder, and I was to come here and wait for him.'

'Well, none of us here know any more than that,' I said. We went into the kitchen. 'The coffee's finished, I'm afraid, but I'll make some more. Or do you feel more like a brandy?'

'Coffee, please, if it isn't too much trouble.'

'I'd put the brandy in the coffee,' Alec said. 'I believe you must be Miss Billson.'

'I'm sorry, I ought to have introduced you,' I said. 'This is my husband, Alec Guest. And this is Detective Sergeant Quarles.'

Nina was still in the sitting-room, presumably telephoning her brother. Imogen was on a chair at the table, looking sulky, as if she did not feel that she was receiving enough attention.

I ground some more coffee-beans and set about making a second jugful of coffee.

Karen spoke to the sergeant. 'I was told to come here, I don't know why. I don't know anything. All they told me is that Nigel's dead and that he was murdered. I don't understand it. And his car's in that garage, that carport or whatever you call it. I don't understand it. It was in the car park at the Green Man last night. Was it stolen?'

'We don't know much more about it yet than you do,' Sergeant Quarles replied. 'Can you tell me what time you last saw the car in the car park?'

'Oh, I don't know,' Karen said. 'Ten o'clock – half past ten – something like that –' She broke off as Nina came into the kitchen.

For an instant the two women stared at one another, then Nina seemed to make up her mind to ignore Karen. She spoke to the sergeant.

'Sergeant, there's something I want to tell Superintendent Berry,' she said. 'I should have told him about it when he was here before. I don't know if it's important. I'm inclined to think it isn't. But still, I know I ought to have told him about it. I just lost my head. But it's possible it's what brought my husband to the bungalow. Will you tell him that?'

'Your *husband*!' Karen suddenly shrieked at her. 'He wasn't your husband!'

Her shriek was immediately echoed by Imogen, who

65

began to hammer the table with her fists and to yell at the top of her voice.

Nina put a hand on her head and stroked it gently.

'Be quiet, darling,' she said softly. 'Please be quiet.'

Imogen pointed an accusing finger at Karen.

'Naughty,' she said.

'All right, I'm naughty,' Karen said. 'But Nigel stopped being that woman's husband weeks ago, and if he hadn't let her divorce him, he could have divorced her and had her name smeared all over the newspapers.'

'Now really . . .' Nina said. 'Aren't you exaggerating? It wasn't a very interesting divorce. You're his latest, I suppose. I'm sorry I used the word husband. Of course it was a mistake. But to keep saying my ex-husband sounds so clumsy.'

Her tone was mild, but there was malice under it.

'Well, I must be going,' the sergeant said. 'And I'll give the superintendent your message, Mrs Elvin.'

Alec saw him out of the house and immediately on his return Imogen cried out, 'Dada! Dada!' and held out her arms to him as if she had been afraid that he might not return to the room.

'A plain case of love at first sight,' Nina said. 'Imogen's always impulsive in her feelings about people. She takes likings to people instantly.'

'Dislikings too,' Karen said sourly.

'Oh, you needn't worry about that,' Nina said, her tone condescending. 'There's nothing rational in the way she reacts.'

'Thank you!' Karen said.

'We haven't introduced you to one another properly,' Alec said. 'Miss Karen Billson – Mrs Nina Elvin.'

The two women stared at one another with what appeared to be cold dislike, then Nina turned to me.

'Veronica, I've just been talking to Raymond. He and Marianne want Imogen and me to spend the night with

66

them. I said we'd do that. I couldn't face our sleeping in that bungalow by ourselves, and I didn't want you to feel you might have to offer us shelter. We've imposed on you enough already. I don't know when these policemen will say we can go, but they can't keep us here forever.'

'Don't worry about that,' I said, though in fact I was a good deal relieved to hear that she had made an arrangement of where she and Imogen should spend the night. I understood her shrinking from the thought of a night in the bungalow, and I was prepared, if necessary, to make up the beds in our spare bedroom and to provide them with supper, but I was very glad that in fact I was not going to have to do this. I felt a great longing to be alone in the house with Alec, neither of us needing to talk, nor feeling that it was incumbent on us to solve a murder. Probably this was a callous way to feel, but we are so used to spending a great deal of our time alone together that the prolonged company of other people can become a surprising strain. Meanwhile, it was time that I began to think of lunch. I had some steak and some kidney, which I thought I could make into a steak and kidney pie, and there was some ice-cream in the freezer which I thought Imogen would like. She had become quite quiet, watching everything that was going on as if she understood it.

Karen had just sat down at the table and taken a packet of cigarettes out of her handbag.

'Mind if I smoke?' she said, and without waiting for an answer, stuck a cigarette between her lips, took a lighter out of her bag and flicked it on.

But before she could light the cigarette, Nina said violently, 'Yes, I do mind! I don't want the air poisoned for Imogen.'

'Oh? All right, have it your way.' Karen replaced the cigarette in the packet and put it and the lighter in her handbag. 'Some people are so funny. Nigel smoked like a chimney, I never saw it did anyone any harm.'

'Not one of his more attractive qualities,' Nina said. 'How long had you lived with him?'

'That's nothing to do with you, is it?' Karen replied. 'You and he'd broken off long before I ran into him.'

'So you didn't even know him very well,' Nina said.

'Oh, pretty well, I'd say.'

'Did you know why he came to my house last night?'

'Didn't even know he'd gone there at all till this morning.'

'Didn't you know he'd gone there in his car. Why did he do that?'

'I couldn't say.'

'Or won't say.'

'Look, the last I know about that car was that it was in the car park at the Green Man, like I told the sergeant.' Karen fidgeted, wanting her cigarette. 'My guess is it was stolen.'

'Why should anyone steal a car to drive from the Green Man to my house?' Nina asked.

'Because he was going on somewhere else, and Nigel saw him take it out of the car park, and he followed him to your house and caught him doing whatever it was he was trying to do there, and so he was murdered. Doesn't that make sense to you?'

Nina was silent for a moment, a rather puzzled look appearing on her face.

'D'you know, that's just what I've been thinking myself,' she said to Alec and me.

'But what about that man you saw him walking past your house with?' I asked. 'And by the way, which way were they going, towards the Green Man or away from it?'

Nina seemed to have to think this over, as if she had forgotten that she had ever seen Nigel and a strange man walk past her house, or at least had forgotten telling us about it.

Then, giving a slight start, as if the memory had suddenly come to her, she said, 'Oh, towards it, away from the village.'

'What man's that?' Karen demanded.

'Oh, don't you know?' Nina said. 'Wasn't he with you at the Green Man?'

'No one was with us at the Green Man,' Karen said.

'Nigel hadn't an appointment there with anyone?'

'Not that I know anything about.'

'So perhaps you didn't really know him as well as all that,' Nina said with mockery in her voice.

'No one knows everything about anyone else,' Karen said. 'But he hadn't an appointment with anyone. He'd have told me if he had.'

'He told you everything?'

'Near enough.'

Nina gave a little laugh, then said, 'But I like your theory that the car was stolen, and that Nigel got killed because he caught the man doing it. I suppose the man was after my jewellery, though the only person who could have told him about it was Nigel. It's very puzzling.'

Alec strolled to the window and glanced out. 'Looks like rain,' he remarked, as if he had grown tired of the argument. But then he turned and went on, 'We must ask Berry sometime if the murder could have been done by a woman. We've been speaking of a man all the time, but perhaps it was a woman.'

Karen jumped up from her chair and began to shout, 'If you're saying I did it –!'

Imogen interrupted with a howl.

Karen went on shouting, 'You're mad! You're crazy! I loved the poor devil!'

Imogen went on howling and for a minute or two there was no point in anyone trying to say anything rational. Then all of a sudden, for no apparent reason, there was silence in the kitchen. It was curiously eerie.

To break the silence, I said to Karen, 'I don't think any-one's thought of your having done it. Now, I'm going to get on with some cooking, so suppose you all go into the sitting-room.'

It felt very peaceful in the kitchen once they had all gone, but I did not immediately get started on my cooking. I went to the window, as Alec had before me, and stood gazing out at our neat but perhaps unimaginative garden. The rain that he had forecast was just beginning to fall. A few drops had struck the windowpane and from the darkness of the sky it looked as if this was a mere beginning. So there was not much hope that I would be able to do any gardening that afternoon. That depressed me, because the weekend, when Alec did not have to go into his office, was the only time in the week when we were able to work in the garden together. But how absurd it was to be thinking of such a thing when there had been murder only across the road. I turned away from the window and began to assemble the ingredients for my steak and kidney pie. I enjoy making pastry and that morning it helped to take my mind off the tragedy that was so close to us.

But for whom was it really a tragedy? It could hardly be one for Nina, who had done her best to sever all links with the dead man. And Imogen had certainly no memory of him. But perhaps for Karen, that rather strange young woman, it was really as much a tragedy as she had been prepared to let it appear. Yet for some reason I felt doubtful about this, though I did not know why. Absent-mindedly rubbing butter into the flour, I tried to sort out my feelings about her. It would have been natural to feel sympathy for her and not much else, yet the sympathy which I certainly did feel was corroded with suspicion, and that was not really typical of me. Alec, who as a solicitor can be chillingly unimpressed by the supposed virtues of other people, tells me I take far too many of them on trust. He says I trust people out of sheer laziness. It requires an effort

70

to doubt people. He is probably right. But that morning, at least, I found myself making the effort even though I wanted only to think about my pastry and my steak and kidney.

When the pie was at last in the oven, I went through to the sitting-room and said that I thought it was time for sherry. Alec got a bottle and glasses out of the cupboard, then went out to the kitchen to fill a mug with some orange juice for Imogen. She was plainly surprised and delighted by what appeared to be an unexpected treat, and gave Alec a smile that would have seduced an anchorite. What surprised me was to find that Nina and Karen were sitting side by side on the sofa and appeared to be engaged in a low-voiced conversation. A peace of some sort had evidently been made between them. But they sprang apart, spilling some sherry, as if there had been something furtive, something suspicious about their having made friends, when the doorbell rang.

It was Detective Superintendent Berry and Detective Sergeant Quarles whom Alec brought into the room. They were offered sherry, but it was refused, whether because of that old story that policemen do not drink on duty, or because they would have preferred something stronger, I did not know.

'I'm sorry to trouble you again so soon,' Berry said, 'but I think you may be able to be of some help to us, if you don't mind answering a few questions.'

He was very smooth, looking around the room with grave good humour. I expected him to want to question us one by one in some other room, but he accepted Alec's invitation of an easy chair near the window, while the sergeant went to sit on an upright chair near the door.

'Miss Billson, there are one or two things I'd be grateful if you'd tell us,' Berry went on. 'You are of course not obliged to do so if you don't wish to, but it would probably save time and trouble if you would.'

'All right, get on with it,' Karen said.

'Well, first of all, what brought you to Maddingleigh yesterday? You came of course to join Mr Elvin, but had you any particular plans?'

She gave him a hard stare, as if she suspected a trap in the question, then she shrugged her shoulders.

'We were going off to Devon for a weekend,' she said. 'Not for any special reason, but just for a bit of time off. I'd a few days' leave owing to me from my job, and we thought we'd give ourselves a nice weekend.'

'Ah yes, your job,' he said. 'Now just what sort of a job is it?'

'I work in a beauty salon,' she answered. 'Gervase Ltd, in Bolt Street.'

'In Bolt Street – well, that's interesting. Is that why Mr Elvin had the address of an hotel in Bolt Street in his pocket?'

'Could be, though I wouldn't have thought he'd have needed to write it down.'

'Quite so. Well, you came down to Maddingleigh after lunch, didn't you?'

'Yes.'

'Why didn't you come with Mr Elvin in the mornin?'

'Because I always work Saturday mornings. I came a soon as I'd had some lunch.'

'But why did you stay in Maddingleigh instead of going on into Devon?'

She gave a quick glance at Nina, which had a look of apology in it, as if she did not want to damage a new-found friendship.

'Nigel wanted to stay until he'd had a chance to talk to Mrs Elvin about some books of his she'd got,' she said.

'Then why didn't he?'

'Why didn't he what?'

'Talk to Mrs Elvin.' He turned to Nina. 'Were you inaccessible all the afternoon?'

'Books!' Nina cried. 'Those damned books! He didn't want any books. These are what he wanted.'

She slipped her shoulder-bag from her shoulder, pulled the zip open and, for the third time that day, poured a cascade of jewellery out of it.

There was silence in the room for a moment, then the superintendent murmured, 'Well!'

He leant forward, picked up a necklace that looked like diamonds with one finger and looked at it with interest as it dangled there.

'Real?' he asked.

'Oh yes,' Nina said.

'And you told Sergeant Quarles there was something you wanted to tell me about, that you ought to have told me about when we were here before. Could this be it?'

'Of course it is. I said nothing about it because I was confused and scared. I thought if you knew I had anything like this you'd think it was what brought Nigel to my house. As a matter of fact, I thought so myself, and I still think so. But it doesn't have to mean that I murdered him to protect them, and of course you ought to know about my having them. So I'm sorry I didn't tell you about them before.'

'But you think they're what brought him to your house?'

'That's more likely than that he came late in the evening to collect some books, isn't it?'

'Yes, I agree, more likely. But doesn't it give you a motive for killing him? What's made you change your mind about that?'

'Superintendent Berry,' Alec said, 'you don't happen to have told us if this is a crime that could have been committed by a woman.'

'Oh yes, by one who was angry enough, or frightened

enough,' Berry said. 'Were you angry or frightened, Mrs Elvin?'

'No. I was sound asleep. And I agree with Miss Billson about what happened. I think a man stole Nigel's car out of the car park at the Green Man, and Nigel saw him do it and followed him and found he was coming to my house. And of course he knew why he was coming, and tried to stop him, because he wanted this jewellery for himself, but he wasn't a strong man, you know. He wasn't at all muscular, and if they had a fight, it would have been easy for the other man to stab him and kill him.'

'Then he didn't go into the house to get the jewels,' Berry said. 'He just went away. He didn't even take the car.'

'He must have been too frightened at what he'd done.'

'Well, it's an interesting theory,' Berry said. 'And it implies, doesn't it, that he probably lives, or has head-quarters of some sort, in this neighbourhood. May I ask, Mrs Elvin, how this very beautiful jewellery came into your possession?'

'My first husband gave it to me,' Nina answered. 'I think he inherited it from his mother.'

'And we now have to decide what we're going to do with it.'

She began to pick it up, to return it to her bag, but he put a hand out quickly and stopped her.

'I'm afraid I can't let you do that,' he said. 'We shall have to take it with us. We'll make an inventory of it, and we'll give you a receipt, but I'm sure you can understand, it would be unfortunate if it were to happen to disappear in the next few days, or if what actually appeared when it was wanted wasn't quite the same as what's on that table. I'm sorry about it, but I've no alternative.'

'Oh, I don't mind about that,' Nina said. 'Take it and welcome. I'm sure it'll be as safe in your hands as in the bank.'

'Thank you,' he said. 'It will have to be tested too, to see if it's as genuine as you think it is. But now let me ask you one thing more. This man you say you saw going towards the Green Man with your husband, who I suppose is the person whom you suspect of having attempted the burglary, how did he know that you had these jewels? How did he know you'd have them here last night?'

'All I can think of is that Nigel told him about them, not realizing that the man would try to take over his crime.'

'Yes, that sounds reasonable.'

At that moment a very distressing thought came into my head. It was that the potatoes and cauliflower that I had left on the stove to go with my pie would be simmering themselves to a mush if I did not do something about them pretty quickly. I said, 'Excuse me for a moment,' and hurried out of the room.

Imogen trotted after me, clutching the mug that had contained the orange juice. When we arrived in the kitchen, she held it out to me and said, 'More!'

'Oh, my dear, what you might be able to tell us if only you knew a few more words,' I said. But I did not think that she could really have seen anything of the fight, or whatever had happened. Her little room, I happened to know, the room decorated with a dado of rabbits, and which opened out of the one that was going to be Nina's, had a window overlooking the garden at the back of the bungalow, not the carport.

She repeated, 'More!' impatiently, and I partly filled the mug with the orange juice, then turned to the stove. I was only just in time. The potatoes looked as if it might be advisable to mash them, though they had not wholly disintegrated, and the cauliflower was about ready. I drained it and put it in a dish which I put into the plate-warming drawer at the base of the stove, then got to work, mashing the potatoes. I heard the policemen leaving presently, shown out by Alec who then came into the kitchen to see what I was doing.

I was making the white sauce for the cauliflower at the time, and this seemed to amuse him. He came behind me, put his hands on my shoulder and kissed the back of my neck.

'How many murders would we have to have to stop you making the appropriate sauce?' he said.

'Well, it takes your mind off things,' I answered. 'I assume they're staying for lunch.'

'The policemen? No, they've gone.'

'No, I mean Nina and Karen.'

'Yes, they're staying. I asked them to stay. I hope that's all right.'

'Oh yes. I was taking it for granted.'

'But Raymond's coming over afterwards to collect Nina and Imogen. She told you, didn't she, that they're going to stay with him and Marianne?'

'Yes, but what's Karen doing?'

'Going back to the Green Man. Veronica, I'm worried about that girl.'

'So am I, but only because she's the type one automatically worries about. Have you any special reason for worrying?'

'It's only a feeling, perhaps rather like yours. But I can't help believing she knows more about what's happened than she's letting on. And that might mean that she's dangerous to someone. I haven't any idea whom, but it could mean she's in danger herself. I've been thinking about that since Nina said she saw a man with Elvin. What do you think about him?'

'I haven't really been thinking about him.' I added a little more milk to the sauce, which was becoming too thick. 'The only person her description has made me think about is Giles.'

Giles, it may be remembered, was the young man who worked for Vic Ordway in his shop in Gaysbrook.

'Giles!' Alec said. 'But didn't she say he was short? Giles isn't exactly short.'

'No, but if you saw him beside Nigel Elvin, who was unusually tall and very thin and somehow elongated, mightn't he strike you as short? Not that I'm suggesting Giles is a murderer. He's always seemed to me a very nice young man.'

'Lots of murderers are said to strike people as very nice. But what would Giles have been doing, going to the Green Man. Oh, of course he needn't have been going as far as the Green Man. He could have stopped off at Vic's. But if he came out from Gaysbrook to see Vic, which isn't at all unlikely, wouldn't he have come by car? He wouldn't have been walking up the road with Elvin.'

'No, of course he wouldn't, and I don't imagine for a moment the man *was* Giles. I simply said he was the only person I'd been able to think of who more or less fits Nina's description. I'm quite sure the person whom the police have got to look for doesn't belong to these parts at all. Probably he comes from London and followed Elvin down here for reasons we know absolutely nothing about. Something perhaps connected with that hotel in Bolt Street. Garnish's Hotel, wasn't that it? And that's partly why I feel that Karen may know more about the whole affair than she's letting on. The beauty salon for which she works is in Bolt Street. Now, I'm going to lay the table. Perhaps you could go into the sitting-room and tell them that lunch will be ready in a few minutes.'

'Bolt Street,' Alec said thoughtfully. Then he bent down and took the mug away from Imogen and took her hand. 'Come along, we're going to look for Mum.'

She went with him readily enough and I finished stirring the sauce and poured it over the cauliflower.

My pie was a good one, I am ready to assert, but no

one except Imogen ate much. And we were all more or less silent. Imogen enjoyed the ice-cream that followed the pie and asked for more, but Nina put a gentle hand on her head and said, 'You've had quite enough already, darling. Veronica, thank you for being so good to us. You must have been working terribly hard.'

I did not deny it, but I did not say that I had worked hard deliberately to achieve a little peace of mind. They helped me clear the table and stack the dishwasher. Then I made coffee and we all went back to the sitting-room, where we were no sooner comfortably seated with our coffee-cups before us than Karen burst into violent tears. She did not merely sob and let the tears stream down her cheeks, she held her head between her hands, shook all over and produced a choking scream. The sound was horribly close to laughter. It was the first time that I had ever seen a person in a good old-fashioned fit of hysterics.

Naturally, Imogen joined in. She was very scared. Nina gathered her up in her arms and held her close. I did not know what to do. I had never had to treat anyone for hysterics and simply sat still, looking helplessly at Karen and hoping that if one did nothing at all the fit would come to an end of itself. That was actually what happened. First the shrieking stopped, then she fumbled in a pocket for a handkerchief and began not very effectively mopping at the tears, and as these slowed down the trembling gradually lessened, to be replaced by such total limpness that it would be easy to believe that she had fainted.

Then she stuttered, 'I'm sorry — so s-sorry. I don't know wh-what came over me.'

'Would you like some brandy?' Alec asked. He looked as helpless as I was feeling.

'Y-yes, p-please, if it isn't a bother.'

He got up to get the brandy. Karen gave a deep sigh and pulled herself upwards in her chair.

'I've never done anything like that before,' she said.

'I don't expect you've ever had a boyfriend murdered before,' Nina said.

Her voice was cold and she was looking at Karen with a good deal of contempt. The slight friendliness that I had thought I had seen developing between them seemed to have disappeared.

'I don't know what to do,' Karen said in a voice thickened by her tears. 'I've lost my job, I haven't much money. I've given up my room, I suppose I'll have to stay here till the inquest, but I can't tell them anything, I don't know anything. Oh, I don't know what to do.'

'You've given up your job, have you?' Alec said. 'But wasn't this just a holiday you were taking, a long weekend?'

'No,' she wailed, 'it was going to be much more than that. We were going to get married, then look for a nice cottage to settle in, where Nigel would do his writing, and we could have children. It all seemed wonderful and I was very happy. Only he said he had this job to do first, collecting his books, because he said they were the only things he'd ever owned and he couldn't bear losing them. And he told me to go to bed and not worry about him, because he didn't know how long he'd be. And I went to bed and to sleep and never knew anything was wrong till that waiter told me.'

'Your plan wouldn't have worked out if children are important to you,' Nina said in the same chill tone as before. 'He'd no use for children. He'd a right to come and see Imogen once a week, but he never came once from the day we broke up.'

'That's different,' Karen said.

'What's the difference? Imogen was his child, wasn't she?'

'No, she was yours, she was yours!' Karen cried wildly. 'And from one week to the next, she'd have forgotten him. He wouldn't have meant anything to her, even if he

79

took her toffee every time. What's the good of that? He wanted children who would really be his own and love him.'

'Like his books,' Nina said sarcastically.

'All right, like his books,' Karen said. 'People get to love books, don't they? I've heard they do.'

'Are you sure it was his books he wanted here, not a nice necklace or two, not to mention some rings and some bracelets? He always wanted to get his hands on that jewellery.'

'And just how was he going to do that? Break into your house and hold a knife at your throat and threaten to kill you if you didn't give the things to him? You know, if it had been you who was found dead I'd be ready to believe he was after your jewellery, but you're alive, aren't you, and he's dead.'

Nina answered with a long sigh. Then she said in a gentler tone, 'I'm sorry, Karen. Yes, I'm alive and he's dead. And perhaps he only wanted his books, and someone stopped him. We oughtn't to be fighting, you and I. It's my fault. I'm sorry.'

Karen gave her a wary look, then after a moment held out a hand. Nina took it in one of her own.

'Perhaps there wouldn't have been a marriage,' Karen said in a subdued tone. 'Perhaps there wouldn't have been any children. I didn't want them unless we were properly married. I didn't want to be a one-parent family. Perhaps he didn't mean half the things he said. I didn't really know him very well. I just loved him, but I'm not sure how much I understood him.'

'That happened to me a long time ago,' Nina said. 'I was almost as young as you and I loved him very much. And the understanding came only bit by bit. That's what would have happened to you if he'd lived. It would have come and you'd have been very unhappy. I'm not really

80

so very sorry for you. When you've got over the shock you may find you're better off than you think.'

Karen gave her another of her dubious, almost suspicious looks.

'But what am I going to do?' she said, a sound of sobs in her voice again. 'See if I can get my job back? See if my room hasn't been let already? Or am I going to be one of the homeless unemployed? You had money of your own, you never had to worry about that sort of thing. You'd lots of money, hadn't you?'

'A fair amount,' Nina admitted, 'and it was probably my main attraction.' She gave the girl a long, speculative look, as if she were wondering what her attraction had been, in what way she could have been useful to Nigel, because she could not believe that he would have fallen in love with a pretty, simple girl unless there was something to be got out of it by him.

At that moment the telephone rang.

I was nearest to it and picked it up.

'Veronica Guest speaking,' I said.

'Veronica,' came Vic Ordway's familiar voice, 'are the police bothering you a lot about the murder in that bungalow across the road from you?'

'A fair amount,' I said. 'But how did you hear about it?'

'Oh, the police came in to see me this morning,' Vic answered. 'Asked me a lot of questions. They'd heard I was acquainted with Elvin. Someone in the Green Man told them they'd seen us talking together. So he was stabbed in the back, was he?'

'I think it more or less describes what happened,' I said.

'Well, I can't say I'm sorry,' Vic said. 'I'm practically certain he was involved in the theft of my Tompion.'

'Well, let me know if I can help in any way,' Vic went on. 'I don't seem to be able to settle down to anything here. Is that girl still with you?'

'Karen? Yes, she's here,' I said.

'I'd get rid of her if you can. I don't trust her.'

'At the moment I don't much trust anybody.' But I was sorry I had said that. All the voices in the room had stopped and everyone was listening to me. 'I expect we're all in much the same state of mind,' I added, hoping that would make it sound merely general.

'Well, as I said, let me know if I can help,' Vic said.

I thanked him and he rang off.

As I put the telephone down a small hand reached up and picked it up. It was plainly a favourite toy of Imogen's. She clapped it to her ear and shouted, ''lo, 'lo!'

'Imogen, put that down!' Nina exclaimed, suddenly sounding angry. She leant over, took the telephone away from the child and slammed it down on its stand.

Imogen began to wail. 'Want phone! Please – want phone!'

'For heaven's sake be quiet,' Nina said fiercely, 'you aren't at home now. Don't make yourself a nuisance.'

'Go home?' Imogen asked hopefully.

'Yes, when Uncle Raymond gets here to pick you up,' Nina answered. 'Not that it's home we're going to. Veronica, I'm really sorry she's being such a nuisance.'

'I think she's doing pretty well,' I said. 'Things must be very puzzling for her.'

Imogen corroborated that they were by letting out another of her shrill cries of woe.

'Has she any toys over at the bungalow?' Alec asked. 'If you'll tell me what she might like I'll go and see if I can find it.'

'That's very good of you,' Nina said. 'Now let me think. There's a teddy bear in a pink knitted sweater that's a particular favourite of hers, and I know it's been unpacked because she took it to bed with her last night. I shouldn't think the police would object to your removing that, even if you aren't allowed to touch anything else in the house. And there's a toy dog, a sort of poodle, which was in her room when I saw it last. It's got a squeak when you press its middle. I think she'd like that too.'

'I'll try to find them,' Alec said, and went out.

Nina had taken Imogen on to her lap, where she was playing with a small pendant on a gold chain that Nina was wearing and for the moment was quiet.

'Have you any children of your own?' Nina asked.

'No,' I said.

'I just wondered. Of course, if you'd had them they'd probably be grown up by now.'

'That's one of the things it's hard to realize. One's imaginary children stay young forever.'

'You wanted them then, did you?'

I found it hard to answer that question. In the early days of our marriage we had wanted children, but all I had ever achieved were three miscarriages, the last of which had nearly killed me. So after that it had really been a relief that there had been no more of those futile pregnancies. But Alec and I had never really discussed the matter, and just what our failure had meant to him was something that I did not honestly know. We had had each

83

other, that was what had always seemed most important to me, and I hoped that it had to him.

'I suppose so,' I said. 'That's normal, isn't it?' I did not want to discuss the matter.

But she went on, 'It's the one thing in life I ever really wanted. I was a very spoilt child myself, and anything I said I wanted I was given. I got so used to that that I took it for granted. My father was in banking and we were pretty well off. Then I married a nice man – he was a successful doctor – and I thought that of course we'd go ahead and have children. But they didn't come. He had me examined and I was told I was perfectly normal and there was no reason I shouldn't have a child. He was the trouble. He was infertile. And the trouble was, I loved him very much. I loved him but I desperately wanted children. Really for the first time in my life I discovered what it was like not to be able to have something I wanted. I don't know what I should have done about it if my husband hadn't been killed in a car accident. I think I was on the edge of a breakdown. And when he was killed I actually went over the edge for a time. I think I was quite mad for two or three months. It was guilt, of course, because I was glad he'd been killed. But that was something I wouldn't admit to myself at the time. It was only later that I started to understand it.'

'You could have adopted a child,' I said, 'if it meant so much to you.'

'That wouldn't have been at all the same thing. No, what I did in the end was marry Nigel. That was crazy enough. But he gave me Imogen, if he gave me nothing else.'

Karen suddenly joined in the conversation. 'And are you glad he's dead too?'

Nina started, then gave a sardonic smile. 'D'you know, I haven't got around to asking myself that. I must give it some thought. But the two cases are quite different. I'd managed to get rid of Nigel simply by divorce and I'd no feelings of guilt about it whatever. The day I got my decree nisi was one of the happiest days of my life. If I'd tried to stay with him any longer than I did I think I'd have gone really mad, but I didn't have to. I was free. It was wonderful.'

'What made you marry him?' I asked. I was thinking that a young woman with her amazing good looks and plenty of money could surely have picked a husband who had more to offer than Nigel Elvin.

She gave a slight shrug of her shoulders.

'You might not think it, but when he chose he had extraordinary charm. And he was so different from nearly all the people I knew. He could be witty, or loving and tender, or amazingly cruel, just as the mood took him. And I found that terribly exciting. And he didn't remind me at all of my first husband. That was important. I'm not sure why it should have been so important, but it was, and for a few months I was deliriously happy. Then that cruel streak that I mentioned began to seem pretty horrible. I felt horrible in myself because I'd liked it. But by then I was pregnant and did everything I could to keep very calm and live a healthy, quiet life. I found he was nicer to me if he had affairs with other women, so I encouraged them. And of course, when the time came, I'd loads of evidence for the divorce.'

'You devil!' Karen had sprung to her feet, had taken a step forward and stood over Nina and the now drowsy Imogen with a look of fury on her face that made me think suddenly how easy it would be to feel afraid of her. 'You drove him to it, did you? You never loved him. You cheated him and drove him out.'

'Perhaps I did,' Nina said thoughtfully, 'though not until he'd cheated me. Anyway, it's all over now. We needn't fight about it.'

'It isn't over. It'll never be over.'

'It's over for me,' Nina said. 'It was over the day I got my divorce. Of course, I'm sorry he was killed –'

'Are you?' Karen cried. 'You're not, you're glad. And you'll be glad to see some wretched creature sent to prison for it.'

'I'll certainly be glad if they find who killed him. I'd nothing against him once I was free of him.'

'You're glad,' Karen repeated, but this time it was in a mutter, and she sat down again, leant back and closed her eyes. The argument seemed to be at an end and in fact none of us spoke any more till Alec returned, carrying a teddy bear in a pink knitted sweater and a small woolly poodle.

Imogen greeted them with a cry of joy, climbed off her mother's lap and took her toys to the hearth rug in front of the empty fireplace and began to give them what seemed to be a lecture on their behaviour. The poodle squeaked in answer, which made Imogen smack him, while clasping the teddy bear to her bosom.

'That was really good of you, Alec,' Nina said. 'Thank you.'

'They were examined most carefully before I was allowed to take them away,' Alec said. 'Which reminded me that if you're going to be spending the night with Raymond and Marianne you're going to need some clothes and they'll probably be given a going-over like these toys before you're allowed to remove anything. They're searching the place very thoroughly. They were particularly interested in the drawer in your kitchen table. It seems Elvin was stabbed with a big common-or-garden kitchen knife and someone had the bright idea that it might come from your kitchen. But when they looked in the drawer they actually found two big kitchen knives there. You didn't normally keep three, I suppose.'

'Oh, don't,' Nina said. 'It isn't a joke. What would I be doing with three big knives?'

'I'm sorry, I didn't mean it as a joke,' Alec said. 'I was just going on to say that it shows they haven't ruled you out as a suspect. People don't usually wander around carrying big knives stuck into their belts, not in this neighbourhood at this day and age, but that's what someone seems to have been doing if the knife that killed Elvin didn't come from your kitchen drawer. I thought I'd just prepare you for the questioning they may be going to put you through sometime soon.'

'I see.' Nina gazed vaguely before her, then gave a little shake of her head. 'It doesn't really make sense, does it? I mean, I'd got rid of him quite effectively. The law did the job for me. I didn't need actually to kill him. Of course, if I hadn't got the divorce . . .' She gave a bitter little smile. 'I really don't know what I might have done.'

'Poison,' Karen said. 'You'd have used poison. And you'd have planned it carefully and you'd have got away with it, and you'd have married a third time. You hate men, don't you? That first husband of yours, you say you loved him but you were glad when he was killed. You weren't anywhere near, were you, when he had that car crash?'

'Oh, for God's sake!' Nina said disgustedly. 'Veronica and Alec, you've been awfully good to me, but I'm longing for my brother to come and take me away. Away from that girl. I'm sorry for her, of course, but she's a little too much to put up with.'

In fact, Raymond and Marianne did not come for nearly another half an hour. We spent most of it in silence, except for Imogen, who suddenly took it into her head that I should play hide-and-seek with her and went and concealed herself behind the sofa. I managed to take a very long time finding her, and when I did so greeted the discovery with exclamations of surprise. She then indicated that it was Alec's turn to hide, but he stuck at that, insisting that he was too tired for anything so energetic.

Thwarted, she returned to her toys on the hearth rug, but when Raymond and Marianne appeared, she ran to meet them with evident pleasure. They both had a bewildered air of distress and both kissed Nina with an air of warm sympathy and Raymond kept an arm round her as she stood up, preparing to leave.

'We'll have to go to the bungalow,' Nina said, 'because I'll need a few clothes. I hope the police aren't going to be difficult about my taking a few things away.'

'They seem very busy over there,' Raymond said. With his face as close to Nina's as it was, the resemblance between them became very marked, though his seemed commonplace compared with hers. 'They don't mind your leaving?'

'I don't think so.'

Marianne had gone to the window and was looking out at the bungalow and the men whom she could see there.

'You know, I can't help wondering what Nigel was doing there yesterday afternoon,' she said. 'You remember, I saw him go in and come out again after a few minutes. If he was simply looking for Nina he could have found out at once that she wasn't there and could have come straight out again. Or if he thought of waiting for her to turn up, he could have stayed a bit longer. It's odd really, isn't it?'

'Yes, and if he'd gone to collect those books of his,' Raymond said, 'it would have taken him quite a bit longer, even though they'd been unpacked and Marianne had put most of them on the bookshelves there.'

'Oh, it couldn't have been the books he was after,' Marianne said. 'He hadn't got his car. He wouldn't have intended to carry them away in his arms.'

'I hadn't really thought about it,' Nina said, 'but you're quite right, it's a bit odd.'

'He didn't leave a note for you, or anything like that?' Raymond asked.

'No.'

'And if he just wanted to see you for some reason, he would have come back later.'

Karen interrupted, 'He went into Gaysbrook to meet my train in the afternoon. That's why he didn't come back later. Actually, I think it's obvious what happened. He took it into his head that he'd look in on Mrs Elvin to arrange about picking up the books, found she wasn't there, thought he'd wait for her for a little while, then after two or three minutes decided he couldn't be bothered to wait and came out again. It's quite simple.'

'Did he tell you he'd tried to see my sister earlier?' Raymond asked.

'No, and as a matter of fact, this is the first I've heard of it,' Karen answered. 'It was just something he did on impulse and then thought was a bore and so didn't even think of telling me about it, because it wasn't important.'

I decided to take a part in the argument. 'I've just had an idea of what might have happened,' I said. 'Suppose he went into the kitchen, when he found the house was empty, and helped himself to a knife and took it away with him. Then later in the day he met this man Nina saw him with and he let him see the knife. Then they went together to the house in the evening, meaning to collect the jewellery, and they took the knife so that they could deal with Nina if she woke up and caught them. But then this man thought he'd like the jewellery all to himself, got hold of the knife and killed Nigel on the spot. Doesn't that deal with everything?'

It produced a silence which for some reason pleased me.

Then Raymond said, 'You aren't serious.'

'Why not?' I asked.

'Well, what happened to the man when he'd murdered Nigel? He didn't go in and steal the jewellery. He just disappeared.'

'Panic,' I said. 'He may be someone who isn't used to murder.'

'It's quite ridiculous,' Nina said. 'It presupposes that I was in the habit of keeping *three* kitchen knives in the drawer of my kitchen table. Two was bad enough, but really, *three*! Now, you dear people, I think we must be going, with more gratitude than I can say for all the help you've given me. Sometime, when this horrible affair is over, Imogen and I will be moving into the house, and then we must get to know each other properly. But goodbye now.'

Together, with the two Markhams, she and Imogen left.

The rain was falling fairly heavily now, so Raymond picked Imogen up and they ran as fast as they could to where he had left his car outside our gate. Nina ran into the bungalow, and we did not close our door until they had driven off, then we closed it and returned to the sitting-room. We found Karen standing at the window, as Marianne had stood a little while before, looking out at our visitors' departure. She had lit a cigarette.

Turning as Alec and I came back into the room, she said, 'I must be going too. Could you lend me an umbrella?'

'Where d'you want to go?' Alec asked. 'If it's to the Green Man I'll drive you there.'

'No, thank you,' she said. 'A walk will do me good. I really need it, I think. I need to get some fresh air into my lungs after a dose of that woman. And Mrs Guest . . .' she paused.

'Yes,' I said.

'I'm ready to take your theory quite seriously. I think it's a bloody good theory.'

The house felt very silent when everyone had gone. After a few minutes Alec sat down at the piano and began to play quietly. I am not sure what it was, but I think it was Mozart. I sat down in one of the chairs by the empty fireplace and found myself giving a little shiver, almost with a feeling that it would be nice to light a fire there, even if it was only September. I felt very drowsy and might have gone to sleep if Alec had not stopped playing. He got up and came to the chair that faced mine across the hearth.

Stretching out his long legs comfortably, he said, 'I agree with Karen, that really wasn't a bad theory of yours. The only thing that seems to me a bit unsatisfactory about it is the question of why this unknown man didn't take the car. Granted he was in a panic at what he'd done and wanted to get away as fast as possible, why didn't he take the car?'

'Perhaps he can't drive,' I suggested.

'And of course another possibility is that he doesn't exist.'

'I'd wondered about that, but why should Nina invent him? She's the only person who saw him.'

'Perhaps because she murdered Elvin herself.'

'Why should she do that when she'd successfully, legally, got rid of him?'

'Because he was after her jewels.'

'It doesn't seem to me an adequate reason for murder. Suppose he'd managed to get them and had got away with them, she'd have known who'd done it and could have set the police on his tracks. He'd soon have been caught. She didn't have to kill him sometime in the evening, have his body lying out in the carport all night where anyone might have found it, then started her screaming for help in the morning. Altogether a very risky way to behave.'

'So you think the stranger does exist. I wonder if anyone saw him up at the Green Man. I suppose the police have looked into that by now. I wonder whether Vic saw him if he went there for one of his customary drinks. Which reminds me, what had Vic to say when he telephoned?'

I had forgotten by then about Vic's telephone call and

for a moment could not remember what he had said. It had not seemed important.

'Oh, he said the usual things about our letting him know if he could help,' I said. 'And – oh, I remember. He advised us to get rid of Karen as soon as we could. He said he didn't trust her.'

'I suppose they met at the Green Man,' Alec said. 'Well, I don't trust her either.'

'Because of her morals, or because of something more substantial?'

'Because of a sort of feeling I have about her, that's all.' Alec folded his hands together across his stomach and for a moment closed his eyes. It struck me that he was looking more tired than usual. Probably, I thought, I was doing the same. Curiously, now that everyone had gone and we were quiet, the fact that I felt extremely tired had only just made itself felt. All those people, I supposed, had been a kind of stimulus, though they were draining me of energy without my being aware of it.

Alec opened his eyes again.

'What's she doing here?' he said. 'Once she'd got to Gaysbrook, why didn't they simply drive straight on to wherever they were going?'

'Because Nigel had his reasons for staying here, so she more or less had to stay too.'

'And we still don't know what his reasons were. You know, it could have been something to do with the Tompion, couldn't it? But if it was . . .' He hesitated. 'Has it occurred to you that Vic himself could have something to do with the theft of the Tompion?'

'I don't know what you mean,' I said.

'I'm not sure that I do. But suppose he'd arranged for it to be stolen –'

'Not Vic!' I exclaimed.

'Well, just suppose for a moment he did, because according to him things haven't been going well with him lately, and if the clock was removed by someone who'd got a customer set up to buy it, then Vic would get his share of the deal – not as much as if he'd sold it on the open market, but still a pretty good sum – and then he'd have got the insurance too. And the person who might have arranged the whole thing could have been Elvin. If it was, it explains why they both seem to have been at Garnish's Hotel in Bolt Street. Elvin probably knew it well because his girlfriend worked in Bolt Street, and he and Vic could have met there on the Thursday that Vic spent in London. And Elvin probably knew the kind of man who'd carry out the job, and one of them could have been the man whom Nina saw with him.'

'But what would he have been doing here the day *after* the theft of the clock?' I demanded.

'Making sure that Vic was going to pay what he owed him.'

'Is it possible, d'you think . . . ?' I began, then stopped.

'Is what possible?' Alec asked.

'Just that Nigel had nothing to do with setting up the theft, but knew about it, and could prove that Vic had been involved in it, and stayed on here after it to start blackmailing Vic.'

'And so Vic killed him?'

I felt a shiver of cold go up my spine. I wished I had not said what I had.

'No, it isn't possible. Not Vic,' I said.

'As a matter of fact, it strikes me as a very interesting idea,' Alec observed. 'I must think about it.'

But we did not go on talking about it. I think we had both rather frightened ourselves. Alec went back to the piano and I picked up a piece of embroidery on which I worked occasionally, without quite knowing what I should do with it when it was finished. If it was good enough I would frame it and hang it up somewhere on some wall. We spent a quiet evening and went to bed early.

Next morning Alec set off for the office in Gaysbrook and I started on the usual round of household jobs. Usually on a Monday I had the small amount of washing to do of things I do not send to the laundry, but that morning I decided that this could be delayed for a day or two. Although I had slept well I still felt an unaccustomed weariness, a feeling that all I wanted to do was sit in the sitting-room and read a thriller. But I spent a little while, before allowing myself to do this, making preparations for our evening meal, and by the time that I had done that it seemed not unreasonable to treat myself to a sherry. I was settled comfortably in my favourite chair with sherry on a table at my elbow and a thriller from the library on my knee when the front doorbell rang.

I muttered a quiet curse, because I was fairly sure what sort of thing it was likely to be, but I got up and went to answer it. I was not surprised to find Detective Superintendent Berry at the door. His broad, bland face with the slightly bulging grey eyes had a tentative smile on it.

'Can you spare me a little time?' he asked. 'There are a few things that I should like to ask you.'

He made it sound as if it was perfectly possible that I might refuse to let him in and when I showed him into the sitting-room he stood hesitating in the doorway, apparently waiting for me to make it plain that he was not unwelcome.

Before sitting down he went to the window and looked out. A watery sun was shining through hurrying grey clouds. It was not at all unlikely, I thought, that we should have more rain later in the day.

'Nice place you've got here,' he observed. 'I've always thought I'd like to retire to Maddingleigh.'

'Do you live in Gaysbrook?' I asked.

'All my life,' he answered, 'except for some time I spent

in the army. Dull little place, but it's got its points. A very good school for the kids, for one thing.'

'You've children, have you?' I said. 'How many?'

'Three,' he said. 'A girl and two boys. Troublesome the little dears can be too. But the girl's done well at school, got her GCSEs. And the elder boy's coming along. The third hasn't got to school age yet, but he's the brightest of the lot. He'll do all right when he gets there. Have you any children, Mrs Guest?'

I did not want to get involved in another discussion of that subject.

'No,' I said. 'Would you like a glass of sherry, Superintendent?'

'Thank you, I don't mind if I do,' he answered, having taken a glance at my own glass to make sure that I was already drinking and that I did not intend to leave him to drink alone. 'That's a nice kid Mrs Elvin's got. Shame to have got her involved in such a squalid business. Have you known Mrs Elvin long, Mrs Guest?'

'Since Saturday afternoon,' I said as I poured out the sherry.

'You don't say! You and your husband had never met her before?'

I began to guess the direction which his questions might be taking.

'Never once,' I said.

'But you know her brother and sister-in-law quite well, don't you?'

'Yes, like us, they've lived in Maddingleigh for some years.'

'Yet you never met Mrs Elvin.'

I had dropped back in my chair. He sat down facing me.

'No,' I said. 'I don't know why. It just didn't happen.'

'And that means you never met her husband either.'

'No. Not until Saturday morning. He told me, as a matter of fact, that he'd never been down here before.'

'Ah yes, at the Green Man. And would you mind telling me what your impression of him was?'

'He didn't really make much impression of any kind on me, except that he was very long and thin and perhaps a bit quarrelsome. I'm not sure why I thought that, it was just a feeling I had.'

'Perhaps because of what you'd heard about him from Mr and Mrs Markham. You had heard about him from them, I suppose. I mean about the divorce and so on. It seems likely they'd have mentioned that as she was coming to live in the bungalow facing you.'

'Oh yes, they had. I knew they didn't like him.'

'For any special reason?'

'Well, for his infidelities, which seem to have been quite blatant, and I think he used to knock his wife about at times. But that's only hearsay. Naturally I've no first-hand evidence of it.'

'What's your opinion of Mrs Elvin, if you don't mind telling me?'

We were now approaching his real reason for having come to see me, I thought, and perhaps without any really good reason for it, I found myself beginning to feel cautious.

'I think she's a very beautiful woman,' I said.

'Yes, she's that,' he agreed. 'And she's got a temperament too. Plenty of character. And your husband had never met her before Saturday either?'

My reply was a bit stiff. 'You'd better ask him that yourself, hadn't you?'

'I'd sooner not bother him if I haven't got to,' he replied smoothly. Big and burly as he was, he could put on a very smooth manner when he chose. 'Can I ask you for your impression of Mr Ordway?'

'He's an old friend,' I said. Yet as I said it, it occurred to me how little I really knew about Vic. You can be close friends with someone, I thought, without truly knowing anything much about them. Some people can even be happily married for years without knowing anything much about each other. 'He's intelligent, kind, friendly. Not likely to have committed a murder. Superintendent, won't you tell me what it is you really want to know?'

He sipped some sherry. 'Just what you've been telling me, Mrs Guest. I'm interested in your impression of a few of the people who seem to have been on the spot when these crimes occurred. Both crimes. The murder and the theft of the Tompion clock. They may have nothing whatever to do with one another, probably haven't. But all the same I'll be grateful for anything you can tell me about the people who might be involved in either.'

'And is it only me you're questioning, or are you going the round of all those other people too?'

'Oh, going the round,' he answered with a smile. 'Please don't feel you've been unfairly selected to gossip about your friends.'

'You relieve me,' I said. 'Well, what else do you want to know?'

'Your impression of Miss Billson, for one thing,' he said.

'She's a quite bright young thing,' I answered. 'I met her for the first time, as perhaps you know, on Saturday afternoon. I was in the village, doing some shopping, when I met her and Mr Elvin together. I had a coffee with them in the teashop there. And there was something a little odd about that. Mr Elvin said they'd be grateful if I'd tell them one or two things, but when it came to the point they never really asked me anything. I asked them several more things than they asked me. The only thing Mr Elvin asked was whether Mrs Elvin would be moving into the bungalow that day. I began to think that he thought it might be useful to cultivate me as a link with Mrs Elvin, that that might help perhaps in getting her to part with his books, if that was really what he wanted from her. But perhaps it didn't really mean anything much.'

'Well, thank you for telling me about it,' Berry said. 'It's interesting. But the girl herself, what did you make of her?'

'I think she was very much in love with him. And she seemed to be looking forward to marriage with him and having children, which I thought a bit optimistic. On the other hand, I'm not sure it was genuine. I thought it might be an act she put on to impress, as she thought, a group of desperately middle class, respectable people.'

He nodded and said, 'I see.' Then he added, 'And would she be capable of a crime?'

'Murder, d'you mean?' I asked, startled.

'Well, it's murder we've been talking about, isn't it?'

'Why ever should she murder her lover?'

'It's been known to happen.'

I gulped down my sherry. If he had not been there I should have helped myself to some more.

'All right, yes, I think she could commit crimes of some sort,' I said. 'A little picking up of what doesn't belong to her, perhaps, or blackmail on a small scale, if she'd got hold of a titbit of scandal about somebody. But murder . . . ?' I shook my head. 'I can't imagine it.'

'Perhaps you're still finding it difficult to imagine that murder actually happened just across the way from you,' he said. He finished his sherry and stood up. 'Well, many thanks for your help and your patience with my questions. I'll now proceed to my next victim. Mrs Markham, I think.'

'You'll find Mrs Elvin staying with her,' I said.

'Well, it happens she went into Gaysbrook this morning. Not that I expect anything very confidential from Mrs Markham.'

'So you're keeping an eye on us all, are you?' I said. 'Am I being tailed – isn't that the word for it?'

He did not reply to that, but bade me goodbye and departed. It was only after he had gone that I realized how tense I had been all the time that he was questioning me. I wondered if it was conceivable that someone would be following me when I went, as I intended, into Gaysbrook in the afternoon. There was some shopping that I wanted to do in the supermarket. No, I did not believe in the tail. It must have been by chance that someone had caught sight of Nina in the town. After all, why should she be followed?

I had some bread, cheese and an apple for my lunch, then got my car out of the garage and drove off to Gaysbrook.

I did not know that I was driving to the scene of a second murder.

CHAPTER 6

Gaysbrook is an uninteresting little town. It consists of a main street lined with small, uninteresting shops, a railway station, a couple of large car parks, two or three churches, two or three pubs, a library, a hospital, a police station, a bank or two, a collection of council offices and on either side of the main street a sprawl of council houses. One or two small streets lead off the main one, in one of which the Victorian building stands which houses the offices of Hollybrook, Darby, Guest. At one end of the main street there is a roundabout around which a few old houses stand which had once been the core of the town. At the other end of it there is a supermarket where once a week I did most of the shopping that I could not do in the store in Maddingleigh.

It was not yet two o'clock when I reached the town and managed to find a place for my car in one of the car parks. Alec, I knew, would still be at lunch in one of the pubs, perhaps with Vic, though they did not always patronize the same one. I set off for the supermarket, pulling my shopping trolley after me. There was a slight chill in the air, which warned of autumn coming, but the leaves on the trees planted at intervals along the main street had not yet begun to turn yellow. I went into the supermarket and trailed around, helping myself to packets of groceries and to fruit and vegetables that I could not get in the village.

I was coming out of it when I caught sight of Nina just

going into one of the banks. I wondered how she had got there. The police would probably not have allowed her to move her Mercedes, and Raymond Markham took the Markhams' one car into the town to get to his office fairly early in the morning. So Nina had presumably come in by bus, which meant that she had been in the town for some time, as our bus service is unbelievably poor. There are two buses in from the village in the morning, one home in the afternoon and another in the early evening. If I had known that she would be wanting to come into the town that day I could have offered her a lift. And I could offer her one home now, if she should want it. I paused outside the bank, wondering whether to wait for her and make the offer, because if I did not the probability was that she would have to wait for the four o'clock bus and it is not very easy to find entertaining ways of passing the time in Gaysbrook. But when I had waited uncertainly for a few minutes outside the bank I began to think what a foolish thing it was to do. She might be inside for half an hour or longer. She had only just opened an account, I remembered, and might well be having a talk with the manager. Turning towards the car park, I began to stroll along slowly, looking at the shop windows as I went by.

I paused longest, as I usually did, outside Vic Ordway's antique shop, looking to see if the Graystan vase with which I had fallen in love was still on a shelf that I could see inside the shop. It was a charming thing of clear glass with blue and white decoration. I had once gone into the shop and asked the price of it, and was told by Giles, who was in charge of the shop at the time, that it was a hundred and twenty pounds. That is relatively inexpensive as antiques go these days, but still I had not had quite the courage to bring my cheque book out of my handbag. One day I would, I was sure, if someone with more courage than me did not snap it up beforehand.

Suddenly I thought, why not now?

As the thought came to me, I knew what my response was going to be. I was going to go into the shop straight away and buy the thing. It would cheer me up. I needed cheering up. The events of the last two days had brought about a state of depression of which I could not rid myself, but securing the vase which for some time I had been thinking of as mine would turn my thoughts in a new direction. I pushed the door open and went in.

There was no one in the shop. I had known that Vic would not be there, as he always allowed himself a fairly extended lunch-hour. But Giles, his assistant, would be in charge. The shop did not close in the lunch-hour, because Giles always brought sandwiches and a Thermos of coffee with him when he arrived in the morning, which he consumed in a room behind the shop. That was where he would be now, but he would be alerted to my presence by the ringing of the bell on the door as I entered. I closed it behind me and strolled across the shop towards my vase.

On the way I took a look at an English Delft porringer, in which I did not allow myself to become too interested, because I happened to know that its price ran into several thousand pounds. However, thinking of that made the hundred and twenty that I was preparing to spend seem quite inconsiderable. I reached up for the Graystan and handled it tenderly, thinking that I knew exactly where I would put it on the top of a bookcase in the sitting-room when I got it home.

I am not sure how long it was before I began to wonder what had happened to Giles. Perhaps, I thought, he had fallen asleep over his lunch. I put the vase back on its shelf and went to the door which led into a room behind the showroom. I pushed it open.

I have never been quite sure what happened next. To this day my memory of it has not come back to me. I think I screamed, but I am not sure even of that. Then my consciousness reasserted itself and I found myself staring out of what seemed to be darkness at what had been Giles. He must have been standing at a table and had fallen forward over it, with his arms flung out. His Thermos of coffee had been overturned and the coffee had mingled with the blood that had seeped out of the wound in his back. It had been the sight of that wound, together with the knowledge that it had killed him, that had given me my moment of unconsciousness. The knife was still in the wound. That was why there was not more blood. I would have liked to faint again, and do it properly this time, removing myself entirely from the scene before me until other people had come and cleared everything up. But having arrived at that point I recognized that it was I myself who must take the first steps in the process.

'Giles!' I said stupidly in a whisper. 'Giles!'

It seemed somehow important to speak to him, though I knew that he could not answer, but to have said nothing, to have come and gone like a thief in the night, would have felt somehow intolerably callous. I knew very little about the boy. He was about twenty-three and as far as I could remember had been working for Vic for three or four years. Vic had been immensely pleased with him. He was by nature a very skilled craftsman and had been invaluable in the work of restoring the antiques that Vic picked up at sales dotted about the country. He lived with a widowed mother who worked as a receptionist for one of the local doctors. He was always pleasant and courteous and seemed to love his work.

One of the most horrible things about the next few minutes was that the telephone was on the table over which Giles had fallen, and only a few inches away from one of his outflung hands. I did not think any blood had actually splashed on to the telephone, but there was a smear of it near it, which made me want to vomit. However, the job had to be faced. Wrapping one hand in my handkerchief because of an idea I had that I ought to take pains not to leave my fingerprints anywhere that could be avoided, I picked up the telephone and dialled. It was only after a minute or two that I found myself talking to Detective Superintendent Berry.

I told him where I was and what I had found. He did not waste much time questioning me, but told me to stay in the shop and that he would be round in a few minutes. I found that speaking to him had steadied my nerves a certain amount, but although I was ready to stay in the shop, I did not think that it meant I must stay in that dreadful room with poor Giles. I turned away and went back into the front shop. And then a peculiar thing happened. I noticed something that I had not seen when I first came into it. Lying on the floor under a rather attractive Regency armchair, as if it had been dropped there and forgotten, was an umbrella. It was a colourful one which I could see, even though it was closed, was in panels of dark blue and bright green. In fact, even without stooping to touch it, I was ready to swear that it was mine. The umbrella that I had lent to Karen Billson the day before.

Of course, I could be wrong. When I had bought it at a shop in Gaysbrook during last winter there had been plenty of other colourful umbrellas there, and quite likely there had been more than one in blue and green. But the umbrella that I had lent Karen was the one that was on my mind. And if this one at my feet should in fact be that particular one, then it meant that Karen had been into the shop, probably during the lunch-hour, and had found what I had found.

In only a few minutes Superintendent Berry and Sergeant Quarles arrived. Soon after them a number of other men came, most of them in uniform, but for a little while I was alone in the shop with the two men whom I already knew and who somehow gave me the feeling that we were old acquaintances. They both looked into the room behind the shop, stood there muttering to one another for a moment, then Berry came out while Quarles remained in the back room, as if they were afraid that the dreadful thing in there might get up and walk away if they did not keep an eye on it.

'Can you identify him?' Berry asked.

My voice was hoarse, as if it had suddenly turned into that of an old woman.

'His name is Giles Langtry,' I said, 'and he's worked here with Mr Ordway for three or four years. That's really all I know about him, except that he lives with his mother, who works as a receptionist for Dr Jarvis. I – I don't know anything about his private life.'

'What brought you in here today?' Berry asked, his voice surprisingly gentle.

'Just a thought I'd like to buy something I've had my eye on for some time,' I said. Suddenly I collapsed on a chair and took my head in my hands. 'I knew Mr Ordway wasn't likely to be here, but I thought I could do the deal with Giles. It was just an impulse that brought me in.'

'You didn't see anyone come in or out of the shop before you?'

'No, but there's something . . . Something it's a little hard to understand. That umbrella . . .' I pointed. 'That's mine.'

'Oh yes?' he said questioningly.

'I'm almost sure it's mine, though I didn't bring it in with me today. I lent it, you see, to Miss Billson yesterday when she left our house and went off to the Green Man. You remember, it was raining quite hard, and my husband offered to drive her, but she wanted to walk. What she was doing with it here today I don't know.'

'It isn't raining today,' he remarked.

'No, but it looks as if it might start at any time, doesn't it?' I said. 'Apart from that, she might have been simply going to bring it back to me, but came in here for some reason, and – and found . . .' I could not finish the sentence.

'You think she found Giles Langtry dead, panicked, dropped the umbrella in a state of shock, and bolted.'

'Yes, that's more or less what I've been thinking,' I said.

'Have you any idea what might have brought her in?'

'Perhaps like me, just seeing something she thought she'd like to buy.'

'You don't really think that, do you?'

I drew a deep breath. 'Well, no, not really.'

'What do you think then?'

'I don't know – I simply don't know!' I began to feel surprisingly angry. 'How could I know? Except that somehow it's all connected with the theft of the Tompion. It has to be, hasn't it. But you haven't told me what happened in there.' I nodded towards the door at the back of the shop, which was half open. 'Was it the knife wound that killed him? And when did it all happen?'

He was keeping a curiously penetrating glance on me, which made me shiver, though it was not unkind.

'It's too early for me to say,' he answered. 'The experts will be along any time now. They'll tell us how long ago it happened, and what was done, and whether there's such a thing as a fingerprint to be found, though that isn't likely these days, with all that everybody knows about such things now. But it seems obvious that the boy was killed by a stab in the back with a knife that's sticking in the wound. It looks as if he'd been opening a package that contains some china, or something like that, cutting the string round it. His blood isn't dry yet, so it looks as if whatever was done, it wasn't very long ago. But that isn't my department. Now, can you tell me where Mr Ordway's likely to be at present?'

I shook my head. 'In one of the pubs, having lunch, but I don't know which.'

'That's usual, is it? He goes out to lunch and leaves – or left – the boy in charge?'

'I've heard him say so. Sometimes my husband has lunch with him.'

'Ah yes, your husband. Will he still be out to lunch, or will he be back in his office by now?'

'I should think he'll be in his office.' I was fairly sure of that. Lunch for Alec was a sandwich and some beer, after which he returned as soon as he could to the office for a short period of peace and quiet before the rest of the staff, together, it might be, with a client, came trooping in.

'Then wouldn't you like to get in touch with him?' Berry asked.

I looked at the half-open door, hesitated, then shook my head.

'Not if it means using the telephone in there,' I said. 'I couldn't do it.'

He nodded understandingly.

'Then I think the best thing for you to do would be to go to the police station and wait for me there. I'll want a formal statement from you presently, but meanwhile you can let your husband know what's happened. Bob –!' He raised his voice and the face of the sergeant appeared in the doorway. 'Bob, see Mrs Guest round to the station, will you, and see that a call gets put through to her husband's office. He'll probably want to go round to the station too. And thank you for your help, Mrs Guest. I'm very grateful to you for keeping your head.'

He gave me a sympathetic smile and patted me on the shoulder. I stood up and stumbled to the doorway, outside which a number of men, some in uniform, some in plain clothes, were assembling. There were two or three cars also drawn up alongside the pavement, and an audience of people presumably unconnected with what had happened in the shop, collecting on the far side of the street.

107

To get away from it all, accompanied by Sergeant Quarles, I set off as hurriedly as I could for the police station.

Alec arrived there about a quarter of an hour later. Sergeant Quarles was in the middle of taking my statement and showed that he did not want to be interrupted, but Alec was not in a mood to wait quietly until the job was concluded. He looked at me with what looked like furiously angry eyes, but I knew that what really made them glower like that was anxiety. He demanded to be told why I had been brought to the police station, and Quarles told him pacifically that it had been mainly for my own convenience. I agreed with him, telling Alec that I had been thankful to get away from the shop. But I had to go back to the beginning of my statement to tell him all that had happened. Alec muttered and shook his head and demanded why he had not been sent for immediately to the shop. I explained that I had felt quite unable to pick up the telephone there, and added that the police had probably not wanted any unnecessary fingerprints on it. He grunted and said that it was a bad business, with which Quarles agreed.

'Giles!' Alec said. 'About as harmless a lad as you could find anywhere. You've no ideas yet about what happened, I suppose.'

'It's a little too early for that,' Quarles said.

'And if you had any you wouldn't tell me,' Alec stated, I am sure correctly, though Quarles only answered with a slight shake of his head and indicated that he would like the rest of my statement. I had lost the thread of it by then and found it difficult to go on. I had just reached my noticing of the umbrella that was probably mine. Alec seemed about to interrupt for a moment, but then remained silent and I managed to go on. A witness was brought into the room to see me sign the statement, then the sergeant asked me to excuse him, saying that Superintendent Berry would probably soon be along, and left us alone together.

I took a look round and said, 'D'you think this room is bugged?'

It was the superintendent's office that we were in, a square, formidably tidy room, furnished with a desk, some chairs, a bookcase filled with what looked like reference books and some more shelves filled with files. It had a window that overlooked the main street, and grey linoleum on the floor.

'Does it matter if it is bugged?' Alec said. 'Is there anything that you want to say to me in confidence?'

'No, you've heard nearly all of it by now,' I said. 'I don't think there's anything I want to add.'

'But whatever made you go into Vic's shop at all?' Alec asked. 'That's the part I don't understand.'

'It was just an impulse,' I said. 'You know that Graystan vase I've told you about. I suddenly thought I'd go in and buy it. I've always known I'd buy it sooner or later, and something about what's happened during the weekend gave me the feeling that that was the time to do it. I wanted cheering up and I thought it would feel fine to have the vase. And now of course I'll never have it, because even if these awful things get sorted out I think it'll always have the smell of blood.'

'It would probably fade with time.'

'D'you think so? I can't imagine it somehow. Alec, I think walking in and finding poor Giles is the worst shock I've ever had in my life.'

'Worse than finding Elvin?'

'I wasn't alone then. What I wanted to do was run away, as Karen obviously did, but a bit of me told me I'd got to get the police.'

'You're sure that umbrella is yours and that it means that Karen was in the shop at some time after Giles was killed?'

109

I lifted my hands in a gesture of uncertainty.

'I *think* the umbrella's mine. And I think Karen must have been in there, though I haven't any idea why. Only somehow it seems to me . . .'

'Yes?' Alec said as I paused.

'Oh, only that all the things that have happened are somehow concerned with the theft of the Tompion. Giles must have known something about it, don't you think?'

'It does seem probable. And Karen's involved in the theft, or at least knows who is. I suppose she couldn't actually have done the murder.'

'That man Berry didn't say if a woman could have done it. But if she had, she wouldn't have left the umbrella behind, would she?'

'You don't know what shock might have made her do. Your first murder must be quite upsetting.'

'Your first murder . . . Then you're sure she had nothing to do with Elvin's.'

'I'm assuming she hadn't, but I may be wrong. But the death of Giles does seem to make it clear that Elvin's death had something to do with the Tompion. Perhaps he simply knew too much about it. If Vic had anything to do with it, as we were saying yesterday is just possible, there might have been a simple matter of blackmail. I wonder if anyone saw Vic go in or out of the shop today.'

'They'll be trying to find witnesses to that, won't they? Just anyone, not necessarily Vic. I should say it's the first thing they'll do. And that reminds me . . .'

'Yes?'

'Oh, it's stupid of me, it's just that I happened to see Nina in Gaysbrook this afternoon. She was going into the bank. But I don't see how she could have anything to do with the theft of the Tompion. Nothing she's ever said or done suggests that she could have. I think the police will be more interested in where Vic had his lunch.'

But that was something that Detective Superintendent

Berry did not impart to us when presently he arrived in his office. He only told us that we were free to leave when we wished and thanked us for our help. Alec thought at first that he would go home with me, but then asked me if I minded the thought of going home alone as there was work to which he ought to be attending in his office. I hated the thought of going home alone, but I was determined not to show it. No one, I was sure, was going to murder me and I had no good reason for expecting that I should find any more corpses. I was very calm and rational about it, went to the car park, got into my car and started the drive home.

I had only just turned out of the main street when I stopped. I was opposite a bus stop and there was a straggling queue of people along the pavement, waiting for the bus that sooner or later would take them to Maddingleigh. In the queue I saw Karen Billson. She looked listless and absent-minded, as if her thoughts were on something far away. She had not seen me yet.

My first impulse was to drive straight on, then I hesitated and gave a little toot on my horn. I was not sure what I meant to do, but it felt impossible simply to leave her there in the queue. She heard the toot, turned her head and saw me.

In a moment she had wrenched the car door open and scrambled in beside me.

'Going to Maddingleigh?' she demanded. 'Then you can give me a lift.'

'I don't think I can,' I said. 'I'll give you a lift to the police station, if you like. They want you there.'

She put a hand on the door handle and began to open the door.

'I'm not going there,' she said. 'If you don't want to take me to Maddingleigh, that's all right, but I'm not going to the police station.'

'Where are you going then?' I asked.

'Perhaps to the railway station. Perhaps to London. It's nothing to do with you.'

'I wish it weren't,' I said, 'but I found the body not long after you. You shouldn't borrow umbrellas if you're just going to leave them about.'

'That damned umbrella!' She had closed the door again and sank back in her seat. 'I was going to bring it back to you. Look, if you take me to Maddingleigh you'll at least know where I am. If I get out here, I'll just disappear in the crowd and you won't be able to find me. What I want to do is get to London, but I want to get my baggage, and you can tell that to the police. They can come and find me. You needn't get into any trouble for giving me a lift.'

As a matter of fact, it had been in my mind that I might get into trouble if I helped her to get away when I knew the police wanted her, but there seemed to be some sense in what she had said. I started the car again and in a few minutes we were cruising along the open road that led to Maddingleigh. She turned her head away as if she did not want to talk to me, lit a cigarette and for some time we were silent, though now that she was there in the car with me I wanted to talk to her.

'What took you into Vic Ordway's shop?' I said at last. 'What were you doing there?'

I thought that she was not going to answer, then she produced one of her favourite phrases. 'It's not your business.'

'If that's going to be your attitude I'm going to turn straight round and take you to the police station,' I said. I was not driving fast, but too fast for her to be able to scramble out in safety. 'What took you into Vic Ordway's shop?'

'It was just because I'd got to fill in time till the four o'clock bus,' she answered sullenly. 'The police are keeping hold of Nigel's car, so I couldn't come in and out in that, and I'm not a rich young lady who can take a taxi,

112

like Mrs Elvin. I'd the afternoon to fill in and I was passing Ordway's place and just thought I'd go in and look around, that's all there was to it.'

I was sure she was lying. I thought her presence in the shop must have something to do with poor Giles's death, and perhaps with the theft of the Tompion, though I had no idea what her connection with those events might be. But I said, 'So Mrs Elvin came into town by taxi, did she?'

'Of course she did,' she answered.

'You saw her, did you?'

'That's right.'

'Where did she leave the taxi?'

'I didn't notice.'

'Was it at the bank?'

'It may have been. As I said, I didn't notice. I'd had some lunch in a pub, I forget what it was called, then I went strolling about, and just because I was fed up went into Ordway's shop.'

'And found Giles.'

'Yes, and found him.'

'Had you ever met him before? Did you know him?'

'Never seen him in my life. My guess is that old Ordway did for him. I think he knew a bit too much about the theft of that clock. It was Ordway, I'm ready to bet, who arranged for it to be stolen, and that lad knew it and was putting the bite on him. That's maybe quite wrong, but anyway, it's what I believe.'

'You don't think it was Nigel Elvin who was putting on the bite, as you call it?'

She gave me a quick sideways look.

'Could be,' she answered.

'It's what you really think, isn't it?'

'As a matter of fact, no.'

It was said with firmness and for the moment I believed her. I was not actually convinced that she was right, but I thought it was what she herself believed.

'I wonder how much you really know, Karen, about all these things that have been happening,' I said. 'I've a feeling that you could explain nearly everything if you would, and that you're being a real fool, keeping it all to yourself. You could be in danger, you know. If Giles was killed because he knew too much, and perhaps your Nigel also, what might happen to you yourself?'

She gave me a sour little grin. 'I could tell you who are really being fools, if you'd like me to do that.'

'I'd certainly be interested to hear what you think.'

'I bet you would.' She gave a little chuckle. 'But I only said I *could* tell you, not that I was going to. No, I'm not telling anyone just now, though maybe I'll tell the police by and by. That seems better sense than gossiping to neighbours.'

'You're probably right.'

'Oh, I'm right all right. And being on the look-out, I don't think I'm in any danger. But people are such fools! They don't see what's staring them in the face. Well, thanks for my lift. You can phone the police now that you've done with me, while I'm getting my baggage together.'

As I drew up at the Green Man she skipped out of the car hurriedly and waving a hand to me, scuttled quickly indoors. I drove on the short distance to my house, and, taking my shopping trolley out of the boot of the car where I had stowed it before leaving Gaysbrook, put the car away in the garage and let myself into the house.

I heard the telephone ringing as I opened the door. I hurried to reach it in time, but whoever it was calling me seemed to be impatient, for the ringing stopped just before I reached it. I went into the kitchen and unpacked my trolley there. I tried to think calmly about what Alec and I should have for dinner, but my mind was dazed. The remains of my steak and kidney pie was the only answer I could think of. It would not be a very lavish meal, but there was enough left over from the day before, I thought, to meet our requirements. We should probably neither of us be very hungry. For a vegetable I had some beans, and I could get ahead now peeling some potatoes. I had just begun on this when the telephone started to ring again.

Going into the sitting-room I picked it up.

'Veronica Guest speaking,' I said.

''lo!' a voice screeched in my ear. ''lo! 'lo!'

'Imogen!' I exclaimed.

''lo!' she repeated shrilly.

Then there was a squeal of protest as the telephone, presumably, was taken away from her, followed by a chattering sound of indignation in the background.

Then Marianne's voice reached me. 'I'm sorry about that, Veronica, but the telephone is one of her favourite toys. Luckily she hasn't yet quite caught on how to dial. When she does I'm afraid she'll give endless trouble. But I didn't think you'd mind if she accosted you and she was so longing to have a go at it. Now tell me, is this terrible thing true?'

'About Giles?'

'Yes.'

'Well, I don't know what you've been told, but it probably is.'

'He's been killed, like Nigel, with a knife, and no obvious motive for it? I mean, nothing stolen or anything like that?'

'That's true as far as I know it,' I answered. 'But I don't know anything about a motive, whether or not there is one. How did you hear about it?'

'Raymond rang me up. He was on his way back to the office after having lunch in the Barley Mow, when he saw a crowd outside Vic's shop, being held back by the police, and when he asked someone what had happened, he was told that that boy, Giles Langtry, had been stabbed to death. He asked one of the policemen there if anything had been stolen – I suppose he was thinking of that clock, and wondering if there was any connection – and he was told that it didn't look like it, though it was really too soon to say. But Vic was nowhere around.'

'So he hadn't been having lunch in the Barley Mow,' I said. 'I believe that's where he usually goes.'

'Yes, but there's something queer about that,' Marianne replied. 'He'd actually arranged to have lunch there with Raymond today and then he didn't turn up. Not that that's too extraordinary. Vic can be pretty casual. But he hasn't got the alibi he'd have had if he'd met Raymond, as he'd suggested.'

'An alibi,' I said. That had not occurred to me. 'Do you think he'll need one?'

'Well, won't he?'

'But he thought such a lot of Giles. He was so fond of him. And anyway, he's bound to have an alibi, having lunch in town as he nearly always does, and seeing lots of people who know him. Of course, if he'd come home for once . . .' I paused, a prickly feeling going up my spine.

'Veronica, Raymond said it was you who found the body. Is that true?' Marianne asked.

For a moment I could not answer, then I said, 'Yes, it's true. But how did you hear it?'

'Oh, my dear, it must have been terrible for you. I told you, Raymond phoned me, and he said he'd met Alec going back to his office from the police station, and he told him. But how did it happen? How did you find him? What were you doing in the shop?'

For a moment I considered simply putting the telephone down, because I felt that I could not go on talking, but then another reason for doing just that came into my mind and I said, 'Forgive me, Marianne, I've just remembered that there's another very important call I've got to make. I've been putting it off, but I really mustn't do that any longer. And about what I was doing in the shop, I just

116

went in because I was thinking of buying something. Please give my love to Imogen and tell her she's a very clever girl to be able to talk on the telephone. Goodbye.'

I did not give Marianne any time to say anything more, but rang off. Then I stood there with my hand still on the telephone, trying to screw up my courage to make the call that I ought to have made as soon as I came into the house. That I had put it off, almost forgetting it, was because it meant confessing that I had almost certainly done wrong. It meant telling Superintendent Berry that I had removed Karen Billson from the scene of the murder and left her alone, to do as she liked, in Maddingleigh. It had seemed a not unreasonable thing to do at the time, but now it seemed criminally irresponsible. But making the call had to be faced. I picked up the telephone again and once more rang the police station in Gaysbrook.

CHAPTER 7

'I see.' Detective Superintendent Berry's voice was cool, but did not express what he was probably thinking, for which I was grateful. 'Thank you for phoning.'

That, for the time being, was the end of the matter. But when Alec came home, as he usually did, at soon after six o'clock, and I told him what I had told Berry, he was not quite so ready to leave it at that. He told me plainly what a fool I had been.

'Once you'd got her in the car, you could have turned and driven to the police station,' he said. 'She's going to turn out to be the most important witness.'

'I did think of doing that,' I said, 'but she seemed to have a quite good argument against it. But I suppose my main motive in bringing her back to the Green Man here was that I wanted to get home myself. I don't seem able to stand up very well to horror.'

He relented, put an arm round me and kissed me.

'And you've had more than your share of it,' he said. 'Anyway, they'll pick her up quickly enough when they want to. Now, what about a drink?'

We took the sherry and glasses out of their cupboard and settled down with them in the sitting-room. I had put the remains of the steak and kidney pie in the oven to warm up, and the beans and potatoes to simmer on the top of the stove, and a frozen chocolate gateau to thaw for our dessert, and thought how nice it would have been to have had the time and the energy to make, say, a really good trifle, with plenty of brandy in it, or some profiteroles with a hot chocolate sauce, to which we are both very partial, but which cannot be tossed off in what is left of an afternoon after discovering a murder. A great longing came to me for the everyday life with which I had often been so bored. There was really nothing to compare, I thought, with a housewife's life, regular, undisturbed and beautifully subject to her own control. A few other interests might help to colour it, but it was really a very privileged way of life.

'You say she's going to turn out to be the most important witness,' I said. 'Do you mean more important than me?'

'I rather think so,' Alec answered. 'She discovered the body before you, didn't she? You just happened to report it. She may even have been on the spot in time to see someone come out of the shop.'

'If so, she seems to be protecting that person.'

'Or thinking out how she can make the most of her knowledge.'

'You're thinking of blackmail again.'

'I admit it's something that keeps edging its way into my thoughts.'

'I assume you think it's the same person who killed both Elvin and Giles.'

'It seems probable, doesn't it?'

'Someone with a knack for finding large kitchen knives just when he wants them.'

'Or knives that happen to find him.'

'I don't know what you mean.'

'I'm not sure that I do.'

He really looked as if he was puzzled by what he had just said. There was a frown on his forehead and bewilderment in his dark eyes. He seemed to feel that he had meant something, but had already forgotten what it had been.

'D'you know what I would really like to understand?' he said. 'It's why Elvin and Karen stayed on here on the Saturday night. She'd come down from London and joined him, and according to her they were going to drive on to Devon for the weekend. Well, that can't have been what they were really intending to do, or they would have done it. So we return to the Tompion. That he knew who took it and had decided to see what he could get out of it. And Giles must have known something too. There doesn't seem to be any other possible motive for his murder. But what was Giles doing with his knowledge that made him a menace to anyone?'

'To that unknown man whom Nina saw with Elvin,' I said.

'If he exists.'

'Why should she invent him?'

'Perhaps because she's involved in the theft of the Tompion.'

I shook my head and sipped some sherry.

'She's a rich woman. She doesn't need to dabble in the dangers of crime to be able to live very comfortably.'

'Sometimes criminals want more than comfort,' Alec said.

'Excitement? Thrills? That isn't how she strikes me. But I'll tell you an odd thing Karen said to me. She said people are such fools, they don't see what's staring them in the face. Does that mean anything to you?'

He shook his head. 'I'm sure we're fools, but she's one too if she thinks she can keep some valuable knowledge to herself –'

He broke off as the doorbell sounded.

'Police,' he muttered, sounding irritated.

But he was wrong. It was Raymond Markham.

'Am I interrupting anything?' Raymond asked. 'I don't want to disturb you. But I've had an idea.'

In a way that it had never done before, his resemblance

120

to his sister made a strong impression on me. But what there was about the two of them that made her a very beautiful-looking woman and him an ordinary-looking man I still could not make out. Was it that I was simply too used to him? I was used to his look of placid good nature, I had been for several years. I had never given him much thought. I took for granted that I liked him, but really I knew next to nothing about him, except that he was a good host at little drinks parties, and a useful guest when we were hosts. He had a pleasant smile and an agreeable voice. I had never heard him argue with anyone, or voice strong views about anything. He watched all the sport that he could on television, went jogging every morning before leaving for his office, yet could not keep down the increasing bulge inside his cardigan, belonged to a bridge club in Gaysbrook and liked playing badminton. And that was really all I knew about him, except that his marriage seemed to be a happy one and he was as dedicated to his garden as Alec was to ours. Yet I thought of him as an intimate friend. But how he was likely to act in a time of crisis was something of which I had no idea.

'No, we aren't doing anything,' I said. 'Come in.'

I took him into the sitting-room. However, he would not sit down and would not accept a glass of sherry. He stood just inside the door and looked at us uncertainly.

'I'm going across the way in a minute,' he said. 'But it struck me that possibly you might feel like coming with me. It's because of an idea I've had. You know Nigel said he'd come here to get some books from Nina, and we've all been assuming that was a yarn?'

'Yes,' Alec said.

'Well, suppose it wasn't a yarn. Suppose it was the truth, the literal truth.'

Neither of us spoke for a moment, then Alec said, 'Have you any evidence for that, Ray?'

'None at all,' Raymond said. 'It simply struck me that we might give him the benefit of the doubt and at least take a look at Nina's books.'

'Is she over at the bungalow now?' I asked.

'No, she's at home with Marianne and Imogen,' Raymond answered. 'She's had a rough time. She was picked up in Gaysbrook and taken to look at the remains of that poor devil, Giles. They wanted her to say if he could have been the man she saw with Nigel the evening before he was killed.'

'And was he?' Alec asked.

'She won't say he was or that he wasn't. She says he could have been. But she's gone to pieces rather badly. These last few days have been too much for her. She fainted after she got in. Only for a few minutes, but it scared Marianne and me. We thought of sending for Dr Daly, but then luckily she came to and only began to cry. We dosed her with brandy and Marianne got her to go to bed.'

'How's Imogen?'

'A bit worried, I think. She's never seen Nina upset before. Neither have I, to tell the truth. Even when Matthew, her first husband, was killed, she only went stiff and cold and unapproachable. That lasted for quite a while, and then she suddenly married Nigel. She's really very tough, though she doesn't look it.'

'Does she know you've come up here to look at her books?' I asked.

'Oh yes, she gave me the key to get in. The police have locked it up, of course, and taken the key away with them, but she's got a spare. She tells me I'm not going to find anything, and perhaps I'm not, but I thought it would be worth taking a look round. Books can be pretty valuable sometimes, can't they?'

'But if there were any valuable books there, Nina would know them, wouldn't she?'

122

'I suppose so. Probably. All the same, I'm going to look for myself, and what I wondered, as I told you, is if at least one of you would care to come with me, to be a witness in case I did find anything. Suppose I do, I don't want to be accused of having planted it there. And if there's nothing, then I don't want anyone saying I removed something.'

'All right, I'll come,' Alec said. 'Veronica, coming?'

Of course I went with them.

We did not expect to be long, and we left the light on in the sitting-room and did not bother to lock our front door. Raymond unlocked the door of the bungalow and led the way in. He switched on lights in the hall and the living-room, a room I had known quite well in the days of our old neighbours, but which seemed completely unfamiliar now. In the past it had been furnished with modern furniture, mostly lined oak with legs that were mostly metal and with armchairs covered in plastic. The pictures had been abstracts and there had been two or three sculptures in bronze of figures which with a stretch of the imagination could be taken for the human form. It had not been at all my sort of room, yet I had had a certain affection for it. There were always flowers in it, and books lying about, so that it looked cherished and lived-in.

It was very different now. As the removal men had left it, it looked desolate and abandoned. The furniture was a mixture of Regency, early Victorian and undistinguished reproduction and had the look of having been picked up, at odd times, without much thought having been given to how it would agree with what was already there. It stood about the room in what would certainly not be its final arrangement. A roll of carpet lay down the middle of the room and a jumble of glass and china ornaments stood on a table. No curtains had been put up yet, but several pictures had been hung. I remembered Nina telling me that Raymond had been invaluable, on the Saturday morning, in helping with the hanging of pictures. They were mostly watercolours of quite attractive country scenes. There was also a built-in bookcase on each side of the fireplace, both of which were filled with books. Seeing to that had been Marianne's job on Saturday morning, Nina had told us. But it had not been completed, for there was a packing-case beside one of the bookcases, which had its lid off, and was filled with books. Perhaps we were going to have to stay longer than I had expected, I thought.

'Well, what do we do?'

'Simply take a look at all the books, and see if there's anything that strikes you specially,' Raymond answered. 'Anything about the binding, for instance. Anything that's unusual.'

'Look, what you need here is an expert, not people like us,' Alec said. 'I might recognize say, a folio Shakespeare, but a mere first edition of Dickens or Thackeray would never catch my eye.'

'I know what you mean,' Raymond said. 'But please, all the same, do take a look through the lot, as I'm going to do myself now, and see if there's anything that seems a bit strange. And when you've given them a once-over, there's something else you might do.'

'What's that?' Alec sounded suspicious.

'Get to work on the lot, one by one, and see if there's anything *in* them.'

'Ah!' It sounded as if that made better sense to Alec than looking for priceless first editions. 'All right, let's get down to it.' He squatted down in front of one of the bookcases, and started to take out of it one book after another. Giving each of them a shake, so that if some paper had been lodged between the fluttering pages it would certainly have fallen to the floor, he began to look interested in what he was doing.

I went to the bookcase on the other side of the fireplace

124

and copied his actions. Raymond attacked the books in the packing-case, stacking them beside it in a heap on the floor. Nothing slipped out of the books I handled. That was hardly surprising, for most of those in my bookcase were paperbacks, not the best of things in which to conceal a precious document.

After a little while I asked, 'What is it you're expecting to find, Raymond? Some evidence of fraud or immorality that Nigel was using for blackmail?'

'Well, isn't it possible?' he asked.

'I suppose so. It only strikes me that if that was why he was so anxious to get hold of his books, he wouldn't have made quite such a fuss about it. He'd have found some apparently harmless way of getting into the house, and then quietly pocketed the volume he wanted when Nina wasn't looking.'

I stood up and brushed the dust off my fingers. The packing by the removal men had covered the books in dust. I was ahead of the other two and began to take a look around the room, then I wandered out into the hall and from there to the kitchen. As Nina had told us, she had straightened it up at once on moving into the house. Saucepans hung from a row of hooks, cupboards were filled with crockery, the sink and the top of the table in the middle of the room were clean, a light shone in the indicator on the freezer, showing that it had been switched on. The only other room in the house, she had claimed, that had been put completely in order was Imogen's room. I do not know what I was looking for, but I started to move towards it.

Then, before I left the kitchen, curiosity gripped me. I pulled out the drawer in the table in the middle of it and looked inside. All the usual kitchen cutlery was there, wooden spoons and knives and forks and spoons of stainless steel. There was a potato masher and an instrument for chopping parsley. But there were no big kitchen knives, or carving knives. Yet I had heard that there should be two there. Who had removed them?

The answer was, almost certainly, the police. But if they had, what had been their object? Did it mean that they suspected Nina of being concerned in the murder of her husband? And if it was they who had taken the knives, then at least it could not be one of those knives that I had seen sticking in Giles Langtry's back. It was unlikely that Nina herself had been so foolish as to remove the two knives. Yes, it was the police who had taken them. But what did that mean?

I strolled out into the hall, feeling confused and a little dazed. And then I saw something that I had not noticed when we came into the house. It was a grandfather clock. Of course, I knew that it was wrong to call it that, it was a longcase clock. I had not noticed it because it had been set down in a corner of the hall where the open door had hidden it. There was no reason why I should be interested in it. It was not in the least like the Tompion. But still it fascinated me and I was standing looking at it when Alec came out of the living-room.

'Nothing, so far,' he said. 'As innocent a collection of books as I've ever seen. Complete editions of Dickens, Dostoevsky, George Eliot, Hardy, Conrad, Trollope — practically no truck with the moderns, except for a few of the staider thriller writers. And not a letter or any scrap of paper that Elvin's possession of need keep anyone awake at night. You know, Ray, I believe you're going to have to accept the fact that what he was after was Nina's jewellery.'

Raymond had followed Alec out of the room. He looked cast down.

'I suppose you're right,' he said. 'In a way it's a pity. If Nigel had been running a sideline in blackmail, Nina would hardly have been involved. But possibly — just possibly, so a policeman might think — she might have

126

murdered to protect her treasure. However, now that I'm here, I'm going to look around to see if there's anything else he might have coveted. I see you're interested in the clock. He wouldn't have cared about that. I believe she picked it up for about twenty pounds in some sale. If Nigel's been involved in stealing a clock, his standard's apparently a Tompion.'

He went on into the dining-room and Alec followed him.

I did not. I opened one or two doors until I found the room in which Nina had obviously slept during her one night in the bungalow. It was still in the state in which the police had found and left it. The bed was unmade, Nina's nightdress had been tossed across it, a suitcase was open with the look of a few things having been taken out of it, a rug lay on the floor beside the bed. A door leading off the room was open. I went towards it. There was a white-painted crib in the room, a white chest of drawers, a chair, a lot of toys, and the walls were decorated with a dado of rabbits – Imogen's room. I remembered that she had been giving the rabbits names. There was nothing there to steal. I returned to the hall and waited for Alec to join me.

I did not have to wait long. He and Raymond came out together from the kitchen, Raymond with a sour expression on his face, as if finding nothing had been a disappointment to him. I thought that it ought to have pleased him, because the less that there was worth stealing the more certain it seemed that it had been Nina's jewellery that Nigel Elvin had been after. That cleared her of such things as being involved with him at some time in blackmail, or any other sinister activity, keeping the evidence hidden in books or any other good hiding places.

'Well, I'm sorry I bothered you people about all this,' Raymond said in a depressed tone of voice, 'and I'm very grateful to you for your collaboration. I'll be getting home now. Of course, the fact that we didn't find anything doesn't mean that it actually wasn't his books Nigel was after. Perhaps that's all it was. Books to which he was attached. I'd rather like to think so, but it doesn't make sense of his murder.'

We left the house together, and while Raymond got into his car Alec and I crossed the lane and let ourselves in at our gate.

It gave me a little surprise at that point to realize that we had left lights on in the house. There was a light in the sitting-room window and in the hall. As I remembered, we had not expected to be away for nearly as long as we had been. We had also left the front door unlocked. I pushed it open, but then abruptly stood still on the doorstep. Music was coming from the sitting-room. Someone was playing the piano. Schubert, I thought it was.

Alec muttered something explosive under his breath and strode past me. I hurried after him and was in time to see Detective Superintendent Berry get up from the piano stool to greet us.

'I must apologize,' he said. 'I couldn't resist the temptation.'

'I'd say you're welcome, if I understood what you're doing here,' Alec said in a not very welcoming voice.

'I must apologize for that too,' Berry said. 'I had no right at all to let myself into the house. But I arrived here with a few questions to ask you and saw lights on, so as no one answered when I rang the bell, I assumed you'd gone out only briefly and that it would be worth waiting for you. So I waited, ringing the bell two or three times, but still no one came. However, I saw lights on over there in the bungalow, so I guessed that's where you might be, and it occurred to me to try your door and I found it unlocked. And for what I did then I can offer no excuse. I committed trespass.'

'Have you got a search warrant?' Alec asked, but his tone had become more amused than censorious.

'No, indeed,' Berry said. 'Nothing.'

'Well, I'm glad you found a way of entertaining yourself while you waited,' Alec said. 'Did you happen to search the house while you had the chance?'

'Certainly not.'

'You're welcome to do so, if you want to.'

'We can discuss that presently. Meanwhile, if you'd answer the few questions I came to ask, I'd be very grateful.'

'My wife and I will be glad to help in any way we can, but first I think some drinks might help to ease the situation. Whisky? Sherry?'

'You're most obliging. Whisky, please.'

At that point I gave a yelp of horror. All the time that we had been away the steak and kidney pie had been in the oven, and the vegetables simmering on the stove. I ran out to the kitchen, to see how bad the situation was.

The pie was safe, because I had set the oven very low, but the vegetables were beyond saving. The water that they had been in had all steamed away and the bottoms of the saucepans had begun to burn. Taking them out to the dustbin beside the back door, I tipped their contents into it, then put them in the sink and filled them with water, thinking dismally of the scouring that I would have to do next day before I could use them again. Our dinner that evening was going to have to consist of pie by itself, followed by the chocolate gateau from the freezer, which had had plenty of time to thaw. Then I returned to the sitting-room and accepted my glass of sherry from Alec and sat down. He and Berry appeared to have been discussing music, not murder, waiting for my return before settling down to the serious matter of the evening.

A little silence fell on us before Berry opened the subject.

'I believe you are a friend of Mr Victor Ordway.'

I suppose we should have expected it. After Giles's dreadful death, it was certain that Vic would be a centre of interest, yet I was taken by surprise.

'Yes,' Alec said, 'we've been friends for a long time.'

'Do you happen to know where he is now?' Berry asked.

Alec and I exchanged glances, both of us, I think, looking a good deal startled.

'Isn't he at home?' Alec asked.

'No.'

'Nor in the hands of the police?'

'No.'

'And of course not in his shop. Well, I'm afraid we can't help you. We've neither of us seen him at all today.'

'We had a telephone call from him yesterday,' I said. 'That's the last we've heard of him.'

'A telephone call? May I ask what it was about?'

'He asked if the police were bothering us much about the murder, and offered to help us if he could. It was just the sort of thing you'd expect him to say, except that he said he was almost certain that Nigel was involved in the theft of his Tompion.'

'Ah, he said that, did he?'

'Do you think he was right?'

Berry answered with a little shrug of his shoulders.

After a moment Alec went on, 'Can't you find him?'

'No, for the moment he seems to have disappeared. So has his car. He parked it in its usual place in Gaysbrook in the morning and was seen by two or three people in his shop, but so far we've found no one who noticed him leave it. He'd arranged to have lunch with Mr Markham in the Barley Mow, but didn't turn up for it and he hasn't been seen since. We've spoken to the woman who does for him here, and she's got a key to his house and took us into it and there are signs that he came home and left again. A suitcase is missing and so are pyjamas, a shirt or two, shaving tackle, a toothbrush and so on. So it looks as if he took off while he had the chance.'

'But why?' I said. 'I mean, you can't suspect . . .' I stopped there, because it was obvious that he had certain grave suspicions of Vic.

He was not ready to say so, however.

'He may have had all kinds of reasons for going away,' he said. 'It happens that it's occurred at a singularly inconvenient time. What do you know of his relations with Langtry?'

'I think he was very fond of him,' Alec answered. 'He always spoke with admiration of his craftsmanship and said how lucky he'd been to find him to work for him, but there was something a bit more than that in the way he spoke of him.'

'You didn't know the young man yourself then?'

'Only slightly. We'd met him a few times in Ordway's house, and in the shop too, when on rare occasions we happened to go in.'

'What was your impression of him?'

'Of Giles? Oh, that he was quiet, rather shy, eager to be liked. I think intelligent.'

'Would you say he was someone likely to be involved in the theft of the Tompion?'

Again we exchanged glances, then Alec exclaimed, 'Good heavens, no!'

'Do you think Elvin might have been?'

'Now that doesn't seem to be impossible,' Alec said.

'Yet the two murders strike me as being almost certainly linked,' Berry said. 'They were carried out in an identical way and within not much more than twenty-four hours of each other. And there's one thing we know about the situation. Ordway was deeply devoted to that clock of his. If he'd discovered that Elvin was involved in the theft and had somehow learnt from him that Langtry was too, mightn't he have lost his head and taken his revenge on the lad, all the more violently because he'd had an affection for him? Then when he realized what he'd done, he came to his senses and cleared out.'

'So you suspect Ordway of Elvin's murder, do you?' Alec said.

'Isn't it a possibility?'

'Aren't there other possibilities?'

'Oh, certainly.'

At that point I entered the discussion. 'Superintendent,' I said, 'you know we were over at the bungalow when you arrived here.'

'Yes, Mrs Guest,' he said.

'Well, we were taken over by Mr Markham, who wanted us to help him check whether Elvin might have been speaking the truth when he said he'd come there to try to recover some books of his. Markham's idea was that there might have been something of value to Elvin concealed in a book. So the three of us searched through all the books there and we found nothing. But in looking round the bungalow afterwards I came on something that seemed to me strange. In the drawer of the table in the kitchen there wasn't a single big kitchen knife. That's pretty unusual. You keep one handy when you're cooking, for chopping onions, cutting up meat, and all that sort of thing. But, as I said, there wasn't one there. Well, does that mean anything?'

He smiled. 'It does, Mrs Guest. It means that I removed the knives that were there to compare them with the two that were used in the murders. And they told us nothing. All four were different. The one used to kill Elvin was an old knife and very sharp. The one used on Langtry was of stainless steel and looked fairly new. The ones we took from the drawer in Mrs Elvin's kitchen also looked newish and were not very sharp. I'm afraid your discovery hasn't told us anything. It hasn't helped to prove that the murders were done by the same person, but of course doesn't disprove that they were.'

'And you think by Ordway,' Alec said. 'And you think they were because of the theft of the Tompion.'

'Doesn't Langtry's death, following the other, make the theft of the Tompion almost certainly the cause, whatever we may think about Ordway?'

Alec did not answer. Neither did I, though I was inclined to agree with Berry. But his statement did not in any way explain why Nigel Elvin had been killed in Nina's carport. That brought us back to her jewellery, and also to the man she had claimed to have seen with him.

'Well, I mustn't keep you,' Berry said. 'I only came, as I was in the neighbourhood, to ask if you knew anything of Ordway's whereabouts, and to suggest to him, if he should happen to get in touch with you, that it would be to his own advantage to get in touch with us.'

He stood up. Alec stood up too.

'I think, before you go,' he said, 'that it would be a good thing for you to take a quick look over our house. For all you know, we're closer friends of Ordway's than we've admitted. He could be hiding here. And you can look in our garage to see if his car's there.'

'That's quite unnecessary,' Berry said. 'I wouldn't dream of troubling you.'

'We should prefer it,' Alec said.

The two men looked at one another with a wary kind of civility. Neither was sure what to make of the other, but each wanted to remain on good terms with the other. Then the detective gave another little shrug of his shoulders.

'If that's the case, of course . . .' He turned towards the door.

Alec went ahead of him, and I heard the two of them go into the kitchen, then into the dining-room and then up the stairs. I heard them tramping about in the room overhead and then after a little while come down the stairs again. Of course, Berry had known that he would find nothing. He said good evening to me then, and let Alec lead him out of the garage. After a few minutes Alec came back into the house without him. I heard him lock the door and he bolted it too, which was something that we very seldom bothered to do, then he returned to the sitting-room and refilled his sherry glass.

'D'you think he'd actually been over the house before we came back from the bungalow?' I asked.

'Oh, certainly,' Alec said.

'What makes you think so?'

'Well, once he'd taken the unusual step of invading it, and was sure we were truly out of it ourselves, how could he resist the temptation? Playing the piano when he'd done it was good psychology. It made him out as a rather eccentric, but on the whole appealing, character. And it worked, didn't it? We treated him very well.'

'Do you think he really suspects Vic of the murders?'

'Along with several other people we know nothing about, probably.' He sat down. 'Veronica, I've been wondering about something. You brought Karen back to Maddingleigh with you. Did it occur to you to wonder why she was so anxious to get back?'

'To collect her belongings, I supposed, before taking off for London,' I said.

'You really think she expected to be able to get away to London?'

'D'you think she wouldn't have been?'

'I'm sure she wouldn't. But of course she may have thought she would, only I don't think she's a stupid girl, and I think she may be quite accustomed to judging when a situation's dangerous. And the most dangerous thing she could do at the moment is to bolt.'

'Like Vic.'

'Yes, like Vic. I think she's more experience than he has

of the seamy side of things. My guess is that she's sitting quietly in the Green Man, waiting for the police to pick her up, having hidden something, or perhaps destroyed it, before they started seriously to look for her. I haven't any idea what it might be. Some papers, perhaps, that give a clue to how the theft of the Tompion was managed, or to the murders. Something, anyway, that could be fairly easily destroyed, but which it was urgent for her to deal with. I believe it must have been something like that that brought her back.'

'You're just guessing all the same, aren't you?'

'Yes, I'm just guessing. Now, what's for supper?'

CHAPTER 8

Soon after the superintendent had gone, Alec and I had our uninteresting dinner, stacked the dishwasher and set it going, then settled down in the sitting-room for what we hoped would be a peaceful evening. The day seemed to me to have been a very long one and I was very tired. Alec's quiet strumming on the piano nearly put me to sleep. I tried for a little while to work at my embroidery, but I found myself making mistakes which had to be unpicked and I soon laid it aside. But when I did nothing, the scene that I had seen at Vic Ordway's shop obsessed my imagination.

The shock that I had felt then seemed only now to make itself fully felt. As long as I had had to keep on acting I had somehow remained very clear-headed, but now that I had nothing to occupy me, the full horror of poor Giles's death obsessed me. It had the quality of a dream. I lived it all over again as if it was actually happening again, and so singularly clearly that I could almost believe that I was in the midst of it still. Like a dream, it was precise and clear and yet completely nonsensical. Unless someone could explain it to me, I was not going to be able entirely to believe that it had been real, any more than I thought that the face looking in at Alec and me through our front window was real and not simply part of the dream. And after a moment the face disappeared and with that happening it somehow achieved reality. It had been Vic Ordway's face. Then the doorbell rang.

Alec went quickly to answer it. Seated as he had been at the piano he had not been able to see the window and did not know who might be at our door. I followed him out and just before he opened the door, I said softly, 'It's Vic.'

He paused, looked at me with raised eyebrows and when I nodded, made an odd face, partly expressive of curiosity, but also of anger. He did not want his evening disturbed, but at the same time did not want to miss anything that was happening.

He opened the door.

'Can I come in?' Vic asked in a whispering voice, as if he felt that there might be people near him in the garden, or perhaps in the house, whom he did not dare to allow to overhear him.

Alec did not answer, but opened the door wider and made a gesture that Vic should come in. He stepped inside with a look of caution, and Alec closed the door on him. The three of us went into the sitting-room and I did what seemed to me the obvious thing to do. I drew the curtains over both the windows.

Vic, standing near the fireplace, gave a deep sigh and said, 'I'll go away if you want me to.'

He was very pale, his hair was dishevelled and I noticed that a button had come off the jacket that he was wearing. He was trembling a little.

'When did you eat last?' I asked.

'Eat?' he said, almost as Imogen might have said it, learning a new word. 'Oh, eat! I don't know. Breakfast, I think. It doesn't matter.'

'Where have you been?' Alec asked.

'I don't know,' Vic said. 'I began by thinking I'd head for Scotland, and I went north, then that started to seem a damned foolish thing to do, and I turned round and made for London, and then somehow I got here, but I couldn't stand going into my house alone and I thought of you. I've got to talk to someone or I don't know what I'll do next.' He put a hand against his forehead. 'But tell me to go if that's what you want.'

'Sit down,' Alec said, 'and Veronica will get you something to eat. I'd offer you a drink, but it doesn't seem the right thing to do if you really haven't eaten since breakfast. Veronica, what can we give him?'

'Only a ham sandwich,' I said, 'or some bread and cheese.'

'Well, let's give him a ham sandwich, and perhaps some coffee. And then we can listen to what he's really been up to.'

Vic had made no move to sit down, so Alec took him by one shoulder and pushed him into a chair. I went out to the kitchen and got to work with our sliced bread and a packet of cooked ham to make a couple of sandwiches as quickly as possible, while making some coffee. It did not take me long, and when I returned to the sitting-room with it I found that Vic was lying back in a chair with his eyes closed, showing no sign whatever of trying to talk. It was now Alec who was standing near to the fireplace, and was looking down at Vic with the expression on his face that I had seen in the hall, though it was exasperation rather than anger that I saw mixed with the obvious curiosity.

'Come on, wake up,' he said as I came into the room, pushing the tea-trolley. 'Eat and then drink. It'll make you feel much better.'

Vic opened his eyes, then sat up with a jerk.

'This is awfully good of you,' he said. 'Yes, of course I want something to eat. But it's the last thing I was thinking of when I came here. I only wanted to talk, to ask for your advice. There are things I've got to tell you . . .' He broke off and attacked the sandwiches avidly, then with his mouth full, he added, 'Yes, I'll try to tell you everything, but you're going to think I'm mad. Yes, insane.'

138

'I meet some of those in my job,' Alec said. 'You'd be surprised at the number of people who think the law's main responsibility is to support them in their delusions. But unlike you, they don't know they're mad.'

'Don't laugh at me!' Vic exclaimed, reaching for the second sandwich. 'I'm quite serious. I've behaved like a madman all day, that's to say, ever since I saw what happened to Giles. I loved that boy, you know, Alec. If I'd ever had a son, I'd have liked him to be like Giles. Yes, I would. I loved him.'

Alec was taking whisky out of the drinks cupboard. He poured out a drink for himself as well as for Vic, but when he looked at me questioningly, I shook my head. I felt that I had had enough to drink that day, and that whatever Vic might have to tell us, I wanted to be particularly sober when I heard it.

'Where were you when the thing happened?' Alec asked. 'You said you hadn't eaten since breakfast, so you hadn't gone out to lunch.'

'No, I was going to have lunch with Ray,' he said. 'But before it I'd gone to a house where they wanted us to do a clearance job. You know how that works. You make an offer for everything that's in the house, undertake to clear out all the rubbish, and hang on to anything there that's worth anything. Well, there was nothing there worth having and I said I was afraid we couldn't do the job, then I went back to the shop to tell Giles it wasn't on, and I . . . I found . . . You know what I found. And that's when I went mad. I got in my car and took off for Scotland.'

'But why?' Alec asked.

'Because of my guilty conscience.'

'But what were you guilty of?'

'You mean you don't know? You haven't sorted it out for yourself?'

'Something to do with the Tompion,' Alec said.

'Of course it was to do with the Tompion,' Vic answered.

'Hell, I stole the damned thing myself. I'm guilty of fraud. And they're going to think Giles knew it and that's why I killed him. Only you see, I didn't, and he didn't know about the fraud. And even if he had, I don't believe I'd have killed him. I told you, I loved him.'

'"For each man kills the thing he loves . . ."' Alec murmured. 'All right, let's assume for the present you didn't kill him, did you by any chance see anyone come out of the shop when you were returning to it, because it looks as if the murder had only just been done when you got back.'

Vic wrinkled his forehead in a puzzled frown, which made him look even more like a monkey than he usually did. He sipped some whisky.

'I don't know. I don't think . . . Well, there was a woman . . . I thought for a moment I knew her, but she didn't seem to recognize me, so I didn't try to speak to her. She was standing in the doorway as I came along. I couldn't even say she'd been inside, she might just have been looking in through the window, and she walked away before I got to the door.'

'You say you thought you knew her,' Alec said. 'Who was she?'

Vic looked confused, as if he could not remember who the woman had been.

Then he spoke suddenly. 'Oh yes, of course, Elvin's wife. Nina Elvin. Very striking woman. I'd met her once or twice at the Markhams'. But she can't have had anything to do with it. I'm sure she'd never even met Giles. But perhaps . . . Yes, that's an idea. Perhaps she'd seen someone come out of the shop. Yes, get hold of her and ask her that. She might be able to give you a description of him.'

'As she described the man she saw walking with Elvin just before he was killed?'

Vic looked puzzled. 'I don't know what you mean.'

'It's only that I've had doubts from the first about that man's existence.'

'Oh, you needn't have any doubts of that,' Vic said. 'I can tell you who he is.'

Alec looked surprised. I knew that he had never wholly believed that Nina had ever seen the man whom she had described, but had invented him for reasons of her own, probably out of fear of being herself suspected of her husband's murder.

'Well, then who was he?' Alec asked.

Vic did not reply at once. He closed his eyes for a moment, opened them, gazed blankly straight before him, drank some whisky, then ejaculated, 'That's really what I came to talk to you about this evening! But now I'm not sure that I ought to do it. I don't think it's fair on you.'

'Never mind about that,' Alec said. 'You've said enough to have to tell us the rest. He was someone connected with this fraud you were talking about, was he?'

Vic nodded. His face looked extremely sad.

'To go back to the beginning,' he said, and then stopped, as if the beginning was something that he could not face.

'Yes?' Alec prompted him, sounding very gentle. I knew that when he was as gentle as that he was really very dangerous. Perhaps it was part of his legal training, a technique he had learnt for extracting information that he needed, which was being withheld from him.

'Well, the beginning was my general financial position,' Vic said. 'Things have been going very badly for some time. I'm up to my eyes in debt and haven't been able to see my way ahead. As I'm sure I've told you, people haven't got the money these days to make a shop of my kind profitable. Perhaps if I'd brought down my standards . . . But even then, I don't think it would have helped much, and I'd have lost all the pride and pleasure that I've been able to take in my work. So I was thinking of shutting down and starting some new kind of life somewhere abroad. If I did that, I thought, the debts could take care of themselves. That's the real beginning, Alec, when I thought of walking out on debts, cheating a number of people who trusted me. That's where my guilty conscience ought first to have got to work.'

'And then you stole the Tompion from yourself,' Alec said. 'Who put the idea of doing that into your head?'

'As a matter of fact, it was Elvin,' Vic replied. 'I'd met him by chance a month or two ago, after not having seen anything of him for quite a while. We saw quite a lot of each other at one time, when he was doing a series of articles on antiques for some newspaper. He didn't know the first thing about them, and I gave him a certain amount of help. Well, I talked more than I should have done about how things were with me, and he suddenly asked me if I'd still got the Tompion, because he'd an idea of something I could do with it.'

I exclaimed, 'But, Vic, you loved that clock! You always did!'

'I love money too, my dear,' he said, 'particularly when it seems to be unattainable.'

'What was the scheme?' Alec asked.

'Just an insurance swindle,' Vic replied. 'Quite simple. Elvin said he knew of someone who would buy the clock on the quiet at a reduced price, leaving me to claim the insurance on it. The net result was going to be rather more than I could have got for it on the open market, and besides that – oh, the idea of doing it began to take hold of me. I've been paying those premiums for years and getting nothing for them. I couldn't really afford to do it. And now there seemed to be a way of getting something, together with an extraordinary attraction I discovered in the thought of doing something really dishonest. I didn't know I had that in me. And Elvin said he could set it up for me to meet the character who would buy the clock if I could arrange to stay at Garnish's Hotel in Bolt Street.

142

So I did that and I met him. His name, or what he said his name was, was Martin Boyd. And we arranged the burglary for the following night, but Christ, Alec' – his voice rose shrilly – 'I was only thinking of burglary, and even thinking of that makes me feel sick now, but I didn't think of murder! I didn't think of the horrors that have happened.'

'Now let's take one thing at a time,' Alec said. 'You say you can tell us who the man was whom Nina saw with Elvin. Do you mean it was this man you met, Martin Boyd?'

'Of course it was.'

'Does he answer to her description of him? She said he was short and thin and fair-haired and wore glasses.'

'That's him!'

'It could be about half the inhabitants of Gaysbrook too.'

'No, no, it's Boyd. Who else had any reason for being here?'

'What reason had he, once he'd got the clock?'

The look of eagerness that had just appeared on Vic's face faded abruptly. It left him looking dazed and scared.

'You know, that's partly what I came to talk about,' he said. But for the moment he did not seem to want to go on talking. He finished his whisky, then sat looking at the empty glass in his hand till Alec took it from him and refilled it.

'Well,' he said when he had done this, 'what was he doing here?'

Vic gave a slight shake of his head. 'I didn't see him myself. I don't even know for certain that he was here. But when you describe him I feel sure he must have been. But it was Elvin who carried out the job. I don't mean the theft. I don't know how much he had to do with that, apart from bringing me and Boyd together. But it was Elvin who started the blackmail.'

'Blackmail!' Alec said.

'Yes, you see I'd held out, when I met Boyd, for being paid on the spot, before he'd got the clock. I didn't trust him. I thought once he'd got the clock he might simply vanish. I'd still have got the insurance, but that wouldn't have come to any more than if I'd put it up for sale at Christie's, when there wouldn't have been any risk like the one I was running. But once they'd managed the burglary, Elvin came to me and demanded Boyd's money back. He said if he didn't get it the whole story would go to the police. Boyd had covered his tracks, it seemed, and wasn't afraid of getting into trouble himself. But I was dead scared. I wasn't used to dealing with people like that. And of course I hadn't got the money there in the house. I'd opened an account with it in London, and I told Elvin he'd have to wait till Monday before I could give it to him. He was angry, but there was nothing he could do about it. We arranged to meet in London on Monday and that's the last I saw of him.'

'So that's why he stayed on here,' Alec said. 'To get hold of you in the evening and try to get the money out of you.'

Vic put down his glass and clutched his head.

'No, no, that doesn't make sense!' he cried. 'He knew we'd got to meet in London. There was no point in him and his girlfriend staying on here. But since he did . . . Don't you understand, since he did, it gave me a perfect motive for his murder? And it isn't everyone who's going to believe that Giles would have had nothing to do with the burglary and the blackmail. The two murders must be connected, mustn't they? And if I'd a motive for the one, why not for the other?'

I had a feeling that Vic had almost hypnotized himself, if such a thing is possible, into a state of believing that he had committed the murders. He was very pale, with bright spots of red on his cheekbones.

Feeling that something a little practical might help at the moment, I said, 'By the way, Vic, what have you done with your car?'

'My car?' he said in a bewildered tone. 'Oh, my car! I put it in your garage. I hope you don't mind. I thought if I left it in the road the police might spot it, before I've decided what I'm going to do.'

'And you came to us for advice about that, did you?' Alec said. 'I'm sorry, Vic, but I haven't any idea what you ought to do.'

'Oh, what I *ought* to do is clear,' Vic said. 'I ought to go to the police and tell them the whole story. But have I the courage for that? Showing myself up to them as a cheap swindler. Showing what a motive I've got for murder. But isn't that what you think I ought to do? Isn't that what you were going to say before I said it?'

He sounded as if he was becoming angry, ready to turn on Alec for the things that he had not said. Alec gave a sigh.

'I wish I knew how to help you,' he said, 'but I'm not accustomed to this sort of thing. Our firm doesn't handle criminal cases.'

'And you've never met a criminal before, have you?' Vic shouted at him. 'You've never had one sitting in your sitting-room and drinking your whisky! Why did I come here? God knows! I had to go somewhere and talk to someone. But whatever you may think, I'm not a murderer.'

'I'm sure you're not, Vic,' Alec said, 'but you have got yourself in a hell of a tangle. There's only one bright thing I can see at the moment. You haven't applied for your insurance yet, have you?'

'No,' Vic said.

'Well, as long as you don't do that, I don't see that you've done anything criminal. If you happened to want to sell the Tompion privately for less than its value, that's your affair. The only thing you can be accused of, as far as I can see, is wasting police time, which is not such a very serious offence.'

'So you think I ought to go to the police,' Vic insisted. 'But are they going to believe me?'

'I'm afraid I can't penetrate the police mind,' Alec said, 'but I don't see why they shouldn't.'

'Do *you* believe me?' Vic demanded. 'Come on, do you?'

I thought that Alec hesitated very briefly before he replied, 'Yes, of course, Vic.'

Vic suddenly swung round to look at me. 'Do you, Veronica?'

I echoed Alec. 'Yes, of course.'

Vic gave a smothered little giggle. 'What hypocrites we all are! But never mind. I'll go to the police. I'll tell them I'm not a murderer. And I'll tell them where they can probably find the Tompion and I expect I'll spend the night in a police cell. But thank you both for listening to me. And thanks for the food and drink. I hadn't realized how badly I needed it. Now d'you know what I'm wondering?'

Alec shook his head.

'I'm wondering if, when this has all blown over, and I've taken whatever's coming to me, we'll still be friends. But I won't try to get you to say anything about that now. Good night.'

'Good night,' I said, as Alec showed him out.

When he came back I asked him, 'D'you think he'll really go to the police, or will we hear from them tomorrow that he's still missing?'

'What makes you think of that?'

'Just that when people ask you for advice, it's generally because they've already made up their minds what they're going to do, and really only want you to tell them they're right.'

'Suppose you tell them they're wrong.'

146

'Oh, then they just decide you're a fool and that it was stupid of them to trust you. But speaking of fools . . .'

'Yes?'

I had just remembered something. 'When I was driving Karen back to Maddingleigh, she told me that we were all fools and that something was staring us in the face. She didn't say what it was.'

'That young woman knows a great deal more than is good for her. I wonder if she's still at the Green Man, or if she's vanished, as Vic did.'

'She hasn't got a car. It wouldn't be so easy for her as it was for him.'

'What d'you think about the woman whom Vic saw standing in the doorway of his shop? Was it Nina?'

'I'd say yes if I could reason why *anybody* should want to murder Giles. What did his murder achieve?'

'That's an interesting way of putting it. Yes, what did it achieve?'

We left the matter there. We were both very tired and we went to bed soon afterwards. Before I fell asleep I found myself reflecting how never-ending the day had felt and that it was at least something for which to be thankful that it was over. Tomorrow could not be as bad. But were we all being fools, I wondered, missing something that was staring us in the face. And if that applied to people like Alec and me, did it apply to Detective Superintendent Berry?

He was nobody's fool. Karen might be seriously underrating him. I heard Alec moving restlessly about in his bed, unable to sleep, but before long I fell into deep, dreamless sleep from which I did not wake till Alec deposited a tea-tray on the table by my bed and told me that he had already had his breakfast and was just about to set off for his office. It took me a few minutes to remember all that had happened yesterday. Strange things had happened, I knew, but just what they were escaped me when the shock of remembering made me sit up with a jerk and spill some of my tea. What could follow such a day, I wondered. Somehow, I thought, it was essential to hold on to peace. There must be some way of getting back to normality.

Except for my thoughts, the day started normally enough. I went downstairs and made myself coffee and toast. I lingered over it, because there was nothing special that I had to do, and it was half past nine before I went upstairs to get dressed. When I had done that and made the beds and gone downstairs again, it was ten o'clock. My plan for the day was quite clear. I had some veal in the freezer, and I had rice, onions and mushrooms too. All I lacked to make a *blanquette de veau* was some cream, but I could get that at the village store, and I could go down to it straight away. The morning was bright and mild and a walk was just what I needed to keep at bay the thoughts left over from the day before that tended to obsess my mind. Putting the veal out to thaw and wondering if I might find that they still had some strawberries or raspberries in the store, I set off for the village.

The strawberries and raspberries that did very well in our garden were long out of season, but at the store the seasons seemed to have no effect. Somehow things from all over the world found their way to our little shop in Maddingleigh at all times of the year. I thought of how different things had been for my mother when I had been a young child. She had had to queue if she wanted even an onion. I had a dim memory of standing in those queues with her, holding her hand, and her triumph when she had managed to buy a rabbit.

I met Nina in the store, with Imogen clinging to her hand.

Imogen was demanding a particular kind of biscuit to which she seemed to be addicted. She could recognize the packaging, even though she could not read the name.

'Bicky,' she insisted. 'Bicky.'

Nina obediently put a packet of the biscuits in question into her shopping basket and said to me with a smile, 'She's going to be horribly spoiled, that's what you're thinking, I'm sure, but I can't help it. She's all I've got, and biscuits are a pretty harmless taste, aren't they?'

There were no strawberries or raspberries, but I found a nice-looking melon.

'She can hardly get seriously corrupted on them,' I said. 'Are you moving into the bungalow yet?'

'Yes, today,' Nina replied. 'I've got to face it sometime, and the longer I put it off, the more afraid of it I'll get. I admit, I *am* afraid of it. I don't know how long it'll take me to get over the memory of that morning and what I found. But I've been told that it was you who found that poor boy, Giles Langtry. It must have been a very terrible experience.'

She looked sympathetic and concerned. To imagine that she could have been the woman whom Vic had seen standing in his doorway, presumably just a few minutes after having come out of his shop, having stabbed his assistant to death seemed ridiculous in the extreme. Karen seemed a much better suspect. We knew at least that she had been into the shop, and I was sure that there was plenty of violence in her nature. But she seemed to have no more motive than anyone else.

We each made our purchases, then started homeward together, with Imogen in a pushchair, nursing her teddy bear in its pink knitted sweater and crooning a little song to it.

After a minute or two Nina went on from where she had left off.

'I suppose the two murders must be linked, mustn't they? They couldn't be quite unconnected.'

'Well, one hears of copycat crimes,' I said. 'The first one puts the idea of doing the second one into the mind of someone who had nothing whatever to do with the first one.'

'But you don't think that's what's happened here, do you?' Nina said. 'I'm certain the two are connected. And that means, I believe, that you'll find that the Tompion's at the bottom of them both.'

I did not feel inclined to tell her what I knew about the Tompion. Partly this was because what Vic had told Alec and me about the theft had certainly been in confidence, but also because there was a trace of doubt in my mind as to whether it had been true.

'How do you make that out?' I asked.

'Just the one crime following so closely on the other. Of course I believe that what brought Nigel with his car to my house was my jewellery, but I believe what brought him to Maddingleigh was the Tompion. He was somehow concerned in its theft. And then when he got here he heard that I was just moving into my new house, and he'd have guessed that I'd have my jewellery with me, moving it from the London bank to the one in Gaysbrook. And what with it being the weekend and the bank being closed, it happened that he was right, though of course his guess might have been quite wrong. I might have moved it when I opened my account last week. But Nigel was the sort of person who had a knack of being right about things like that. I sometimes used to feel that he knew everything that was going on in my mind and could guess exactly what I was going to do next. I hated the feeling. It was as if I had no private life of my own.'

We crossed the road to the turning that led into our lane. Imogen chose that moment to decide that her teddy bear had committed some offence and began to whack it lustily on its bottom, calling out, 'Naughty! Naughty!'

'But even if you're right,' I said, 'what has it got to do with Giles's murder?'

'Oh, because he knew too much,' she said.

150

'About the Tompion or your jewellery?'

'About both, of course. He was a danger to someone.'

'But he wasn't like that, Nina, he really wasn't.'

'How on earth can you know? Didn't Karen go in to see him? Why did she do that, if it wasn't something to do with those crimes? You know, I don't trust those people whose characters are advertised as being so perfect that they couldn't do anything wrong. It's likely to be just a case of whitewash, if you ask me.'

'All right, suppose he did know something about those things, how did he get to know it?'

'Naughty! Naughty!' shrieked Imogen, and the next moment was holding her teddy bear close to her bosom and kissing it tenderly.

'It could have been in all sorts of different ways,' Nina said. 'I'm not going to try to suggest any. But I imagine he and Nigel must have known each other at some time. That seems obvious. Do you know anything about Giles's past, before he took the job with Ordway?'

'Next to nothing,' I said. 'I believe he grew up in Gaysbrook. You know his mother's a receptionist for Dr Jarvis. Who or what his father was I don't know, but I've an idea the marriage broke up and he went off to London.'

'To Garnish's Hotel in Bolt Street?'

'Nina! What makes you say a thing like that?'

She gave a dry little laugh. 'I don't know. It just suddenly occurred to me. Anyway, the boy was the product of a broken home. That has a way of producing peculiar people. It's one of my terrors about Imogen. I think it'll be better for her being the product of a one-parent family than grow up with a father like Nigel, but still how much better for her it would have been if she'd only had two loving, affectionate parents. I grew up in a broken home myself, but it was Mother who took off with a lover, and left me to the care of a father who never thought of anything but his work and a sister of his who moved in to

151

look after me and never forgave me because she'd given up a career on the stage to do it. Not much of a career it would have been is my belief, or she couldn't simply have given it up, and for someone else's child. I had material things, but not much love when I was a child, and I'm determined that Imogen is never going to go short of it, even if it's got to be in a one-parent set-up.'

'Perhaps you'll marry again,' I said.

'Not me!'

'Why not?'

'When you've lost two husbands you really don't want to risk trying a third.'

'Giles, I've been told, had a very loving mother.'

She gave another of her brief laughs. 'Oh dear, I believe you've been taking me seriously. Of course I don't mean that every child of a broken marriage is going to get involved in crime. He may lead a life of purest virtue, neither murdering nor getting himself murdered. I only insist that Giles *must* have known something about the Tompion and my jewellery, and he was threatening someone about it. There's no other possible motive for his murder. There weren't any women in his life, were there? It doesn't sound like it.'

'I really don't know,' I said. 'There may have been.'

'I suppose we'll hear about that sooner or later. Even if the police don't tell us anything about it, the press will dig it up. We haven't attracted much attention so far, but now that we've got three crimes all together, they're sure to start taking an interest in us. Oh – look at that!'

We were in view of our houses, and in the lane in front of Nina's was a car with two people standing beside it. One was a young woman in jeans and a wind-jacket, with long, dishevelled hair. The other was a young man in clothes almost exactly like hers, but with hair cropped exceedingly short. He was carrying a camera. As soon as they saw us coming they started walking towards us.

'Didn't I tell you?' Nina said. 'The press.'

Imogen eyed them with deep interest. Then as the young man approached her she waved her teddy bear at him and greeted him eagerly.

'Dada! Dada!'

CHAPTER 9

The young man smiled back at her, raised his camera and clicked it.

That was how Imogen first had her picture taken for the papers.

I left Nina to cope with the situation and escaped into our garden. Luckily, the young couple did not seem at all interested in me. Looking back at them as I closed the gate behind me, I saw that they had each taken up a position on a side of Nina, and with her between them, so that they looked a little as if they had taken her prisoner, were marching towards the gate of the bungalow. Leaving her to them like that felt slightly callous, but I did not see how I could help her. I pushed open our front door and went indoors.

I put some bread and cheese on a tray, carried it into the sitting-room and poured out a glass of sherry for myself. Although I had fled from the press I could not stop thinking about them. I sat down, sipped my sherry and wondered what it was about my walk and my talk with Nina that was haunting me. For something was. And suddenly I knew what it was.

I knew the truth.

I knew what had happened on Saturday night in the bungalow. And I agreed with Karen, it had been staring us all in the face.

But I was not prepared at first to admit that it had. Something was surely wrong. But even if it was not, what could I do about it? What could anyone do? Because staring you in the face is not evidence. I went on sipping my sherry and presently eating my bread and cheese and brooding on the impossibility of doing anything useful. For I supposed that it would be useful to unmask a murderer.

It had never occurred to me in my life that I might ever have to do such a thing and I was quite unprepared for the emotions that the thought of doing it roused in me. First and very strongly came the conviction that of course I was wrong and that someone like me simply did not have the mental equipment for solving such problems. Then came an intense desire to talk to Alec, but that would have to wait till the evening. To discuss the matter on the telephone would not do at all. And the evening was a long way off. And then came a feeling that there was something that I could do, although it would probably lead to nothing.

But if it led to nothing it would not actually do any harm, would it? Would it or would it not? It might make me look foolish if anyone understood what I was doing, but that was unlikely. I finished my lunch, took the tray back to the kitchen, let myself out of the house and set off along the lane.

Having committed myself to action, I walked fast. When I let my pace drop, my conviction that I was acting sensibly also flagged and a desire to turn round and go home mounted in me. But in about ten minutes' time I had reached the Green Man and found myself standing at its door, willing myself to go in.

They knew me there, though they were no doubt surprised to see me there alone instead of as usual with Alec. I looked round for Alison, the young woman who was mainly responsible for the bedrooms upstairs, and for the needs of the people who occupied them. She was a tall young woman with a pleasant, friendly face, observant grey eyes and a mop of light brown hair. She was behind the bar when I arrived, helping the barman, Jimmy, but when she saw me she left it to him and came towards me.

She seemed to divine that I had not come for a drink.

'Hallo, Mrs Guest,' she said, 'what can we do for you?'

'Alison, you've a young woman staying here called Karen Billson, haven't you?' I asked.

'That's right,' she answered. 'A terrible thing for the poor kid, that man getting killed. She was crazy about him, you know. And the police keep bothering her, as if she had something to do with it. I don't know why she doesn't go home, though perhaps they won't let her go just yet. She'll have to be a witness at the inquest, won't she? Poor kid, I'm so sorry for her.'

'Yes, well, there's something about her I wonder if you could tell me,' I said, adding untruthfully, 'I don't want to add to her troubles by bothering her, and it's just a small thing.'

'Anything I can do,' Alison said helpfully.

'It's just that she was in Gaysbrook yesterday afternoon and I drove her back here and I tried to get in touch with her after I got home, but she seemed to have gone out. Anyway, they couldn't find her to answer the telephone. Do you happen to know if she did go out?'

'That's right,' Alison said. 'She went out again, almost as soon as she got in.'

'You don't happen to know where she went, do you?' I asked. 'You see, I was expecting her and she didn't turn up. I've been feeling a bit anxious about her.'

Lying does not come easily to me, but when I do it, I try to do it well.

Alison shook her head.

'She was only gone half an hour or so, then she came back and I think she lay down on her bed, but I couldn't say for sure.'

'You didn't by any chance notice when she went out if she was carrying anything?' I asked.

'Well, yes, I think she was. Yes, of course she was, though I couldn't say what it was. Matter of fact, she asked me where the post office was, and I said in the Stores, so I suppose it was something she was thinking of posting, only it didn't look like a parcel she could put in the post. Perhaps she thought they might have wrapping paper and string there, only I don't think they do.'

'Yes, I dare say that was it and she just forgot about coming to me.'

'I think she's up in her room now, if you want to see her.'

'No, I won't trouble her. Thank you, Alison.'

I turned away and started the walk back to our house, but I had gone only a little way and was only just out of sight of the Green Man when I stood still, trying to think something out. Karen, carrying a bundle, had left the pub almost as soon as I had deposited her there, then she had been gone for half an hour and probably had got rid of her bundle while she was gone, since Alison had not mentioned noticing that she had failed to do so. So the bundle had almost certainly been dumped somewhere quite close to the Green Man, not more than a quarter of an hour's walk away. But where could that be?

It was Alec who had put it into my head that Karen's urgent desire to return to Maddingleigh the day before had been to hide or destroy something, and I wished he was with me now to listen to my theory of what that something was. I might wait for him now to discuss it with him. But by the time that he reached home it would be dusk and a search would almost certainly be fruitless. I had to act for myself, and do it now. I had to ask myself where, within a quarter of an hour's walk from where I was standing a good hiding place was to be found, and go there and see if I could find anything. An answer came to me almost at once.

Considering that Karen did not know the district and

must have made use of the little that she had seen of it, it seemed certain that she must have made use of Threadwell Pool. The Threadwell was a small stream about halfway between the Green Man and our house, passing under the road through a small stone bridge and rippling out across a meadow till it came to a basin known as The Pool. A path ran down from one side of the bridge, alongside the stream, encircling the pool, then went on to the village, where the stream, flowing on beyond the pool, filled the village duck pond. The pool was visible from the bridge. If Karen had ever wandered out there she would have seen it and if she had something of which she wanted to dispose, it must surely have occurred to her as just the place for it.

But what was I going to do about it?

I spent some minutes leaning on the bridge and gazing at the pool, wondering what to do. The pool was not very deep, but deeper than I felt inclined to try wading in. Suddenly I made up my mind and set off for home as fast as I could. I went to the shed where we kept our gardening tools and taking out of it a long-handled hoe, returned to the bridge. Descending on to the path beside the stream, I hurried along it till I came to the pool. I had an irrational feeling now that haste was necessary, which was probably no more than an impatient desire to test my own guess, since Karen, the one person whom I did not want to let into the secret of what I was doing, would certainly keep away from the neighbourhood. Reaching the pool, I grasped the hoe that I had brought and started poking and prodding about with it in the water.

I encountered reeds and here and there a tin can and an empty, sodden cigarette package. The bottom of the pool was muddy and my hoe stirred up clouds of mud, but nothing of the kind for which I was looking. I edged my way around it, reaching as far into it as I could. Perhaps, after all, I thought, I would have to try wading. Even

158

if I did not go in very far, it would increase my reach by a little. I paused, rather breathless, contemplating taking off my shoes and tights, when I gave myself one more try before undertaking anything so drastic, and this time suddenly the hoe caught in something. With great caution and a sense of extreme tension, I pulled it towards me. On the end of the hoe was clinging what I had almost been expecting, a child's shoe.

I picked it delicately off the end of the hoe and examined it. It had been white before the muddy water had soiled it, and was a plain model with a strap and a button, but to go by the state of the sole, it had never been worn. Laying it down on the grass, I thrust the hoe in again at about the place where it had caught the shoe. I could feel something there, something soft and heavy. Probably it was only heavy because it was waterlogged, but the hoe would not take hold of it.

But what did that matter? The shoe was enough.

I shook it to get rid of as much water as possible, then started on the short walk home.

When I reached it, I put the hoe away in the tool-shed, then went into the house, spread a sheet of newspaper on the coffee-table in the sitting-room, put the little shoe down in the middle of it, sat down and gazed at it. I had not made up my mind what to do next, and I felt as if the shoe itself, if only I looked at it steadily enough, would instruct me. Perhaps it did, for when I had been sitting there for what felt like half an hour, though it may not have been more than ten minutes, I got up and went to the telephone.

I dialled the number of Hollybrook, Darby, Guest. When the girl at their switchboard answered, I asked to be put through to Alec. In normal circumstances he disliked my phoning him at the office, but circumstances at the moment were far from normal.

When I heard his voice, I spoke rapidly. 'Alec, I've found

out who the murderer is. I've found out when it was done. What shall I do about it?'

'Now wait – for God's sake wait a moment!' Alec exclaimed. 'What d'you mean, you've found out –?' He broke off and in a different voice said, 'Yes, thank you – just put it down there, will you? Thanks.' Someone, it was obvious, had come into his office, and he did not want whoever it was to hear what he had been about to say to me. There was a pause of a moment, then he went on, 'What d'you mean, Veronica?'

'Just what I said,' I answered. 'I can tell you who the murderer is, but it takes a bit of explaining, and I don't think I can do it on the telephone. I can tell you a name, but it won't mean anything to you without the explanation. The question is, can you get home?'

'What, now?'

'Yes, now.'

'You know I can't, unless you give me a bit more to go on.'

'Then ought I to get hold of that man Berry?'

There was another pause, then Alec said, 'Listen, Veronica, is this something you're serious about?'

'Of course I am,' I said. 'I'm deadly serious.'

'I mean, it isn't just a fantasy of sorts, a wild idea you've suddenly thought of?'

'Certainly not.'

'Have you any evidence?'

'As a matter of fact, I have. And I can tell you where there's more to be found. Oh, Alec –!' I think a note of desperation got into my voice. 'Can't you come? I want to talk it over with you, before I go to the police, but I can't put that off much longer. I'll never be able to explain to them why I didn't get in touch with them at once.'

'I see.' Again there was silence for a moment, then he went on, 'All right, I'll come. But this evidence you say you have . . .'

'Yes?'

'Oh, never mind. It's just that I'm wondering if you know what evidence is. Can't you just give me a clue of sorts to the kind of thing it is.'

'It's a shoe,' I said. 'A child's shoe. And I fished it out of the Threadwell Pool, and I'm sure there's the pair to it in there, though I couldn't find it, and some clothes too which I couldn't pull out. But if you like I'll go back and wade in and see if I can get hold of it.'

'Don't touch it!' he said quickly. 'A shoe sounds quite good enough. And if there's more to be found, it'll be best if the police are there to get it out themselves, or at least be witnesses when we do it. So just hold on and wait! I'll be as quick as I can.'

He put his telephone down and with a feeling of reluctance I put mine down too. I did not much like the feeling of being alone, loaded with a terrible responsibility. And now I had to sit and wait till he arrived. I wondered if I ought not to have waited for it, but should have telephoned the police straight away. Ought I perhaps to do that now, so that he and Alec could be there together to listen to my explanations? But I did not really consider that for a moment. I was so used to sharing any problems that arose in my quiet life with Alec that to act now without consulting him would have felt like gross disloyalty.

But I could not settle down. I roamed about the house, went into the kitchen and started peeling some onions for the *blanquette de veau* that I had planned to make in the evening, gave it up because I knew that it would never be made, went back to the sitting-room and sat down, staring at the shoe, picked it up, thinking that I would clean it, put it down again, because I believed it ought to be left just as I had found it, then poured out another glass of sherry and drank it at a gulp. All the time I listened for the sound of the car arriving. When at last it did I ran to the front door and flung it open. But it was not Alec's

161

car, nor was Alec in it. It was Detective Superintendent Berry who was just getting out of it.

'Good afternoon,' he said. 'A nice day, isn't it?'

I had given the weather very little thought since the morning, but looking up at the sky I had to agree that it was a fine, soft blue, while sunshine was brightening the garden. But I was too nervous to say so. I wondered for a moment if Alec had changed his mind about coming home and had telephoned the police for me, telling them that I had something important to tell them. But I dismissed that thought almost as soon as it had occurred to me.

'Good afternoon,' I echoed the superintendent. 'Yes, it's very pleasant.'

'There are just one or two things I wanted to ask you about, if you can spare me a few minutes,' he said.

'Why, of course,' I answered, letting him in at the door and closing it after him. Leading him into the sitting-room I wondered what he would make of the child's shoe on the newspaper on the coffee-table. A shoe on which the mud was beginning to dry. I almost felt that it would be impossible not to tell him what it was doing there, even if Alec had not returned in time to hear it.

'It's about Mr Ordway,' he said, apparently not noticing the shoe. 'I believe he came to see you yesterday evening.'

'Yes,' I said.

We both sat down, and I saw him looking at the shoe, but he did not remark on it.

'We had a telephone call from him just a little while ago,' he said. 'It was from Heathrow and he told us that he was leaving for foreign parts, but he would not tell us where. And he said that if we wanted to know the story of the Tompion, we were to come to you, that he'd told you everything about it yesterday.'

'That's true,' I said. 'At least, I think it is. He told us a

162

great deal. But d'you mean he's just decided to disappear abroad?'

'It looks like it.'

'But that's impossible! What about his house? What about his shop? It's full of valuable things. He can't simply have gone away and left everything behind.'

'I think he has some intention of returning eventually. He said that when we had caught the murderer of Nigel Elvin and Giles Langtry he would return and would face what he had to for his attempt at an insurance fraud. But as long as there was a probability that we would suspect him of the murders, he would remain abroad, he hoped undiscovered.'

'And he told you to come to us?'

'He did.'

'So he expects us to tell you all that he told us.'

'It would seem so. And I'm inclined to wonder why you haven't done so already.' He was still looking at the shoe. He looked as if it interested him deeply, but it was not what he had come to talk to me about.

'Well, it was difficult to know what we ought to do,' I said. 'What he'd told us was of course in confidence. And we didn't even know how much of it was true. He was in a very excited, emotional state, chiefly because he was sure you were going to suspect him of the murder of Giles Langtry. We did try to encourage him to go to you, but I don't think it meant much to him. And if we'd told you all about it ourselves, it would only have been hearsay, wouldn't it? It wouldn't have meant much to you.'

He gave a sardonic smile. 'Ah yes, hearsay. But we could probably have prevented him from going abroad. The fact is, isn't it, Mrs Guest, that you're old friends and you didn't want to get him into worse trouble than he's in already?'

'I suppose so.' I sighed. 'But you don't suspect him of the murders, do you?'

'Our minds are still open on the subject.'

'Have you seen Karen Billson since I brought her out here?'

'Oh yes, she's at the police station at the moment. But she knows her rights when it comes to keeping her mouth shut.'

'You know, I think she knows everything about the murders and the theft of the Tompion and sooner or later she may break down and tell you all about it.'

'More than you're going to tell me, Mrs Guest?'

He withdrew his gaze from the shoe and we exchanged a long look. I began to wonder if he really knew more about the murders than he wanted me to realize, but I did not want to talk about it till Alec arrived. So I returned to the subject of Vic Ordway. I told him all that I could remember of what Vic had told us on the previous evening, first about the man Boyd whom he had met at Garnish's Hotel and whom he believed was the man whom Nina claimed to have seen in the company of Nigel Elvin in the evening before his murder, then about his belief that he had seen Nina standing in the doorway of his shop, though he had not been sure of that, then of Nigel Elvin's attempt to blackmail him. Berry prompted me now and then with a question and when I had come to the end of it thanked me and said that it cleared up a number of things.

'But Boyd isn't the murderer,' he said. 'He almost certainly organized the theft of the clock. Incidentally, we know where it is; in fact, I wouldn't be surprised if those London chaps have got hold of it already. But Boyd spent Saturday and Sunday in a police cell in Hammersmith. They'd had an eye on him there for some time and he's been arrested for burglary and by now has probably been charged. His alibi for the murders is as sound as an alibi can be. So after all we come back to Mr Ordway, don't we?'

'No!' I cried. 'No, we don't! I can tell you what really happened –'

But there I broke off, because I had heard a car outside our door and this time I knew that it would be Alec. I drew a deep breath.

'Yes, in just a moment, when my husband comes in, Superintendent, I'll tell you what really happened.'

Alec came in and as he had already seen the superintendent's car in the drive, showed no surprise at finding him in the sitting-room with me. But his gaze went straight to the shoe on the coffee-table. I had told him that the evidence that I had discovered was a shoe, but I did not think that he had expected the kind of shoe that it was. In fact, he had probably expected, if he had really expected anything at all, a man's shoe.

I did not know where to begin my explanation. The first thing seemed to be to tell Alec why Berry had come.

'Vic has been in touch with the police,' I said. 'He's gone off abroad, but he telephoned them from Heathrow and told them to get in touch with us. He wanted us to tell them everything he told us yesterday. I've been doing that.'

Alec had sat down.

'And that's all you've been doing?'

'That's all,' I said.

'You haven't said anything about . . . ?' He paused and nodded towards the shoe.

'No, I've been hoping you'd get here in time to save me from having to explain my theory twice. And you just have. I was just going to begin. It's a rather urgent matter, because, among other things, Vic has decided to go into hiding until the murderer's been found. He's sure that he's going to be suspected of the murders until that happens. As we know, he's a very frightened man.'

Alec turned to Berry.

'I gather my wife hasn't told you yet that she believes

she's solved the murders. She hasn't told me either what it is she believes. But I gather that shoe there is at the heart of the matter.'

'So I've been assuming,' Berry answered placidly. 'But we hadn't got around to discussing it yet.'

'All right then,' Alec said to me. 'Whose is it?'

'Imogen's, of course,' I replied.

'And it's somehow connected with the murder?' Alec said incredulously.

'Yes, as Karen said, it's been staring us in the face. Nigel Elvin came down here to steal something, didn't he?'

'Nina's jewellery, wasn't it?'

'No, my dear. Nina's child. It was to have been a simple case of kidnapping.'

Both men stared at me steadily. I felt confused, not knowing how to go on. What had seemed to me so clear only a little while ago now seemed desperately muddled. Alec helped me with a question.

'And all they got away with was Imogen's shoe.'

'No, you see the shoe isn't exactly Imogen's. I mean, she'd never worn it. It was part of the outfit they'd brought down for her to wear when they'd got hold of her.'

'You say "they",' Berry said. 'How many people do you presume were in on this?'

'Just the two of them,' I said. 'Nigel Elvin and Karen Billson. Karen was only in it because he needed someone to help him cope with Imogen once he'd got hold of her.'

'But what gave you this idea?' Alec asked, looking very doubtful.

'You did,' I answered.

'I?'

'Yes, you said you'd like to understand why Elvin and Karen stayed on here on the Saturday night instead of going straight on, once she'd arrived here, for that week-end trip they'd been planning, or said they had. And we thought their staying on must have been something to do with the theft they'd been planning, the theft of the jewellery. But I couldn't help wondering what Karen could have to do with the theft of the jewellery. She'd only have been in the way, I'd have thought. Why did he need her? And then this morning it suddenly dawned on me that there was something much more valuable in the bungalow that night than the jewellery, and that that was Imogen. We'll never know, unless Karen can tell us, whether he meant to use the child as a sort of hostage, to get money out of Nina, or simply from sheer possessiveness. Perhaps he wanted her just as Nina wanted her. That's what I believe.'

'But Nina said he took no interest in Imogen once they'd separated,' Alec said. 'He never even came to see her at the times when he'd been given a right to do so.'

'A blind,' I said. 'He didn't want anyone to think he'd any interest in her. But there's another thing you said that suddenly seemed important to me, and that was that Karen's hurry to get back to Maddingleigh yesterday afternoon looked as if there was something she wanted to hide or destroy before anyone else discovered it and it dawned on me later that that could be the clothes they'd have had to bring down for Imogen, because when he snatched her out of her cot he wouldn't have had time to pack a little suitcase for her. He'd have had to try to get her to the car, where Karen was waiting to take hold of her, and get away as quickly as possible. Only of course things went wrong for them.'

'You infer,' Berry said, 'that Mrs Elvin caught him before he reached the car and stabbed him in the back.'

'What else?' I said.

'But this is all speculation,' Alec said. 'I'm quite ready to believe it, but what's the proof you said you had?'

'It's in the Threadwell Pool,' I said. 'That's where I found that shoe. I found out from Alison at the Green Man that when I set Karen down there after I'd driven her back from Gaysbrook, she went out again almost immediately, carrying a bundle, and that she was gone for about half an hour. So I thought of where she could have gone and come back in that time to get rid of her bundle, and my guess was the pool. So I got one of our hoes and I fished about in the pool, and after a time I caught that shoe. I went on fishing for a time, to see if I could find the pair to it, but I only found what felt like a bundle of sodden cloth, which I couldn't pull out. But if you go down there and fish around yourselves, with better implements, I think you'll find a collection of clothes for a young child. And then you can question Karen. She was a witness to the murder. She must have seen Nina stab her husband.'

Alec turned to Berry.

'But could a woman have done it?'

Before the detective had made up his mind what to say, I answered, 'Didn't you say yourself that she could if she was angry enough or frightened enough? And Nina would have been in a truly murderous rage. Because – think of it! – even if she rescued Imogen on Saturday evening, how could she be sure he wouldn't try it again? How could she let Imogen out to play with her friends when Nina couldn't see her? How, if it comes to that, could she ever let Imogen out of her sight for years – yes, *years* – to come? Oh, she could have done it.'

Superintendent Berry spoke gravely. 'But if Karen Billson was a witness to the murder, why has she said nothing about it? Why has she behaved in a way that could easily have made us suspicious of her?'

'I can only guess that she was too scared to do anything else,' I said. 'Kidnapping is a serious offence, isn't it? The kidnapping failed, but even so, being involved in an attempt at it would have seemed to her something she'd at all costs got to conceal. For the same reason, she didn't drive away in the car, but ran back to the Green Man, taking the bundle of clothes they'd brought for Imogen

168

with her. And she got rid of them as soon as she could.'

'If you're right about all this,' Alec said, 'there's still something you haven't said anything about. In the afternoon before the murder Marianne Markham was at the window here and she saw Elvin go into the bungalow, stay for a few minutes, then come out again. What was he doing?'

'You can guess about that as well as I can,' I said. 'I think in the first place he may just have wanted to have a look inside the bungalow to see where the child would be sleeping, and he would have told Nina something about wanting his books. But when he realized that the bungalow was empty and that the door was unlocked, he went in to take that quick look round on his own. And of course he'd have seen that the room with the dado of rabbits and the white cot in it was obviously going to be Imogen's. And he may have done something to the latch on the window, something that wouldn't catch Nina's eye but that would make it easy for him to get in. Only perhaps he didn't realize that there was a door from that room into Nina's bedroom and that it would be open. However quiet he was, and however he managed to muffle the shrieks that Imogen must have tried to give, he was almost certain to wake Nina. And I suppose she was just in time to see him making off towards the car, carrying the child, and realized what he was doing. So she rushed into the kitchen, grabbed a knife and attacked him even before he knew that she had caught him. But you'll have to get all that from Karen. She'll be able to tell you just what happened.'

'But will she be able to tell us why Nina killed Giles?' Alec said. 'Because I suppose you assume she did and that you're going to go on and tell us what made her do it.'

His tone was a little sarcastic, and I could not help feeling that he was wishing that he had thought of my theory himself. In a way I wished that he had. It would have freed me of a frightening load of responsibility.

'I really haven't had time to think it out,' I said. 'I'm sure she did it, and I'm sure she must have been out of her mind at the time. D'you remember, she told us how she was nearly going out of her mind when her first husband was killed? But her only object in killing Giles, as far as I can see, was to make it look as if Nigel's murder had something to do with the theft of the Tompion. It was likely, wasn't it, that it would be assumed that Giles had known something about the theft, and was a danger to someone? To that mysterious man, for instance, who Nina was supposed to have seen with Nigel, and whose existence you never quite believed in. Again, Karen may be able to tell you if that's right. She must have been in the shop almost immediately after Nina. In fact, she may only have gone in out of curiosity because she'd just seen Nina come out.'

'And you think Nina carried carving knives about with her,' Alec said, 'in case she should happen to meet someone she wanted to kill.'

Berry answered for me. 'We think we can explain the knife. It belonged in the shop, so a neighbour's told us, and was used for slitting up the wrapping on packages that arrived there, cutting string and so on. If your explanation is right, Mrs Guest, we must assume that her first murder so unbalanced Mrs Elvin's mind, which was never very stable, that the idea of killing Langtry simply seemed to her a wonderful way of laying a false trail away from her husband's murder. It's possible she looked into the shop and saw Langtry there alone, and the impulse to kill him simply swept her away. Well, thank you, Mrs Guest, for a very interesting discussion. Our next step will certainly be to go fishing in the Threadwell Pool. Meanwhile, if you don't mind, I'll take this little shoe away with me.'

He stood up, stooped over the coffee-table, wrapped the

170

shoe in the newspaper on which I had placed it, said good day to us and left.

We were both silent for some moments after he had gone, then suddenly Alec took me in his arms. I had begun to cry. I hid my face against him.

'Alec, d'you realize what I've done to that child Imogen?' I sobbed. 'Oh God, why did I do it?'

My memories of the next few days are confused. I know that Karen broke down and corroborated nearly everything that I had said. The discovery of the child's clothes in the pool was a great shock to her. She had imagined that they were safe there and would never be found. She was put on probation for three years.

Nina was arrested and some time later was sentenced to be detained at Her Majesty's pleasure. Her mind had been totally unable to support its load of guilt and had become violently unbalanced. At her trial she looked as startlingly beautiful as ever, though with a wildness in her eyes that was frightening. Her jewellery was deposited at her bank and would one day be Imogen's.

Imogen was cared for by the Markhams. She would grow up as their child. It might be years before she learnt anything about her true parentage. What the knowledge would do to her when it came to her, as inevitably it sooner or later was sure to do, I did not like to think. Meanwhile, living in Maddingleigh as she did, we saw a good deal of her. She retained her warm liking for Alec and even when she was old enough to call him by his proper name treated him as if she expected something paternal in his relationship to her.

One day Alec suggested to me that we should remake our wills, each of us still leaving everything that we had to the other, but adding a clause that if we should die at the same time, as is not impossible nowadays for people who use cars or travel in aeroplanes, all that we had to leave should descend to Imogen.

We have not done this yet. I suppose we are waiting to see what kind of person she develops into, but I think that we shall probably do it in the end. We have no close relatives for whom we have any affection, and apart from that I know that I have a lingering feeling of wanting to make up to her a little for what I did to her. I suppose if I had not done it Detective Superintendent Berry would have sorted everything out without my help, and also that being brought up by the Markhams is a better fate for the child than being in the care of someone as crazed as Nina had become. I assure myself of this continually, but a discomfort stays in my mind. When I was a young girl I used to have a daydream of becoming a police woman, but I should not have had the moral stamina for it.

Vic Ordway eventually came home. So did his Tompion. It was returned by the police who had discovered it when they arrested a man called Boyd at Garnish's Hotel in Bolt Street. Vic was not arrested for having stolen his clock from himself. The fact that he had intended to carry out an insurance fraud, but had not got around to doing so, was quietly brushed under the carpet. It seemed a very small thing compared with the crimes that had actually taken place. But he did not stay in Maddingleigh or carry on with the shop in Gaysbrook. The shop is now a women's dress-shop, and has tempting things in its window, but I have never been able to make myself go into it to buy any of the things that I want from time to time. I believe Vic is living in London, but I do not know what he is doing.

Our new neighbours who bought his house after it had stood empty for several months are a pleasant elderly couple with whom we have an excellent relationship. The man is a retired professor of economics from London University and his wife writes romantic novels. I have only one thing against them and that is that they have a longcase clock in their hall. It happens to be the clock that came from Nina Elvin's bungalow, which they bought when its contents were sold up. That did not happen until some time after her trial. Raymond Markham saw to it and also from time to time shows people round the bungalow, endeavouring to make a sale. Just seeing the clock, when we visit our new friends, though it is nothing like the Tompion, brings back unhappy memories and I wish it were not there.

The bungalow stands empty.